'Don't move yet. I'm going out of the front door. They'll rush me then. That's your chance to go out the back way. Got that?'

'Quite clear.'

'Good! But don[...] [...]s of getting out of here [...] [...]urs are one in ten. The[...] [...] compunction if they [...] ...ont know what you're doing he[...] ...it doesn't matter. Make for London. If you get there, tell them what happened.'

From outside came again the wheezing cough.

'That's Goudini,' said Frazer.

Ginger stole a glance at the man whom by this time he realized was a British Secret Service agent. There was nothing in his manner now to show that anything unusual was happening. He was leaning back, smoking a cigarette contentedly, his eyes on the ceiling.

'All set?' he inquired casually.

'All set,' returned Biggles softly. Then to the others, 'You've heard what has been said. Stand by.'

Captain W. E. Johns was born in Hertfordshire in 1893. He flew with the Royal Flying Corps in the First World War and made a daring escape from a German prison camp in 1918. Between the wars he edited *Flying* and *Popular Flying* and became a writer for the Ministry of Defence. The first Biggles story, *Biggles the Camels are Coming* was published in 1932, and W. E. Johns went on to write a staggering 102 Biggles titles before his death in 1968.

www.**randomhousechildrens**.co.uk

BIGGLES BOOKS
PUBLISHED IN THIS EDITION

BIGGLES
in SPAIN

CAPTAIN W.E. JOHNS

RED FOX

Red Fox would like to express their grateful thanks
for help given in the preparation of these editions to Jennifer Schofield,
author of *By Jove, Biggles*, Linda Shaughnessy of A. P. Watt Ltd
and especially to the late John Trendler.

BIGGLES IN SPAIN
A RED FOX BOOK 9781782952107

First published in Great Britain by Oxford University Press, 1939

This Red Fox edition published 2004

Red Fox Books are published by Random House Children's Publishers UK,
61–63 Uxbridge Road, London W5 5SA
A Random House Group Company

Addresses for companies within The Random House Group Limited
can be found at: www.randomhouse.co.uk/offices.htm

THE RANDOM HOUSE GROUP Limited Reg. No. 954009

A CIP catalogue record for this book is available from the British Library.

The Random House Group Limited supports The Forest Stewardship
Council® (FSC®), the leading international forest-certification organisation.
Our books carrying the FSC label are printed on FSC®-certified paper.
FSC is the only forest-certification scheme supported by the leading
environmental organisations, including Greenpeace. Our
paper procurement policy can be found at
www.randomhouse.co.uk/environment

Printed and bound in Great Britain by Clays Ltd, St Ives plc

Contents

Chapter 1
An Interrupted Cruise

Major James Bigglesworth, known to his many friends (and qui e a few enemies) as Biggles, tossed aside the book he nad been reading, and stretching out his arms with a gesture of utter boredom, yawned audibly. The movement caused the deck-chair in which he was reclining to creak ominously; the sound brought a muttered exclamation of alarm to his lips, and he relaxed quickly to his original position. The book lay where it had fallen on the deck near his feet, the pages fluttering noisily in the fresh sea breeze.

'Your book'll be overboard in a minute if you don't look out,' observed Algy Lacey from the next chair of the three that were lined up just abaft the red funnel of the S.S. *Stavritos*. Ginger Hebblethwaite, Biggles' protégé, occupied the third.

Biggles made no movement to recover the book although it was clear that Algy's warning was well founded. 'A watery grave would be too good an ending for such balderdash,' he observed coldly.

'I was told it was a good book,' declared Ginger.

'The fellow who told you that ought to be made to eat it,' returned Biggles, more than a suspicion of sarcasm and bitterness in his voice. 'And the fool doctor who sent me on this crazy trip ought to be made to eat his instruments,' he continued, as an afterthought.

'He said you needed a rest,' reminded Algy.

'I know. I'm getting it. But this life on the ocean

wave bores me stiff. Nothing happens. We go on, and on, and on, and still nothing happens.'

'It is rather a bore, but what do you want the skipper to do—run the ship on a rock or something?'

'That would at least provide a little active entertainment. This sitting here doing nothing all day is giving me the jitters. The one thing I've never been able to do is nothing. I've done that now for five days and that's just about four days too long.'

'Try looking at the sea,' suggested Ginger.

'For what purpose? Do you suppose I've never seen the sea before? The trouble with the sea is that it always looks the same. One wave may be a bit bigger than another, but when you have seen one you've seen the lot. You can have them all, large and small, as far as I'm concerned.'

No one answered, so Biggles was left to ponder on the reason for this unusual voyage. It was a simple one. A recurrence of fever, picked up during one of his trips to the tropics, had sent him, for the first time in many years, to see a doctor for treatment. Every day for a fortnight the doctor had plied him with a concoction of quinine, at the end of which time he announced that his patient was clear of fever, but would profit from a sea voyage.

Ginger, who had done very little sea travelling, voted the idea a good one. Algy had agreed. So Biggles acquiesced, and four days later found them on a Greek cargo boat, homeward bound to Athens, from where they proposed to return by air. Biggles had firmly refused to travel on a cruise ship. They had now been at sea for five days, and Biggles was beginning to find the monotony irksome. The rock of Gibraltar, which they had passed the day before, had provided a brief interval of interest; but now it was far astern, and the next port of call, Marseilles, two days ahead.

Ginger walked to the rail and pointed to a faint smudge on the northern horizon. 'There's land,' he remarked.'It ought to be Spain.'

'It is,' agreed Biggles briefly.

'I wonder how the war's going on there*?'

'That's the sort of thing you *would* wonder about. It would not surprise me if you were also wondering how you could find your way into it.'

'I wouldn't mind having a look at it, anyway,' admitted Ginger frankly.

'Then you can put it right out of your mind, my lad,' said Biggles firmly. 'We've done quite enough barging into other people's wars. So just relax, and thank your lucky stars you have nothing to do but eat, sleep, and then eat and sleep again. Hullo! What's that?'

Biggles and Algy joined Ginger at the rail as the hum of a distant aero engine was wafted to their ears.

'Air France trans-Mediterranean air mail, for a guess,' suggested Algy, shading his eyes with a hand, the better to see the approaching speck.

'It's coming this way,' put in Ginger.

Now, it is a curious thing, but no matter how long a man may fly, however familiar aircraft may be to him, he cannot resist looking up at a passing aeroplane. The three airmen moved along the deck to a position where their vision was not interrupted by the rigging.

'He's certainly coming this way,' agreed Algy. 'He wasn't at first, but I saw him alter his course a little

---

* Spanish Civil War 1936–1939. A war fought in Spain between the republicans, aided by volunteers from many countries, and General Franco and his Nationalist supporters backed by Hitler and Mussolini. Eventually, Franco won.

9

just now. Maybe he's having trouble with his engine. Hullo, he's cut it!' he went on quickly as the drone of the engine died away. 'He is certainly making for us.'

'They evidently think so on the bridge,' observed Biggles, as several orders rang out, to the accompaniment of the engine-room bell.

'They seem to be getting quite excited about it, too,' remarked Algy.

'It doesn't take much to get a Greek excited,' murmured Biggles.

'They are certainly getting worked up about it,' declared Ginger, as a fresh volley of orders was shouted from the bridge. Several of the crew who had been below came bustling up on to the deck. From languid mid-afternoon quiet, the ship had suddenly become a hive of activity.

Biggles puckered his forehead in a frown. 'Yes,' he said wonderingly, staring at the members of the crew, who were running to and fro casting furtive glances upwards, 'I'm no alarmist, but this begins to look more like panic than excitement. What's the idea? I fancy there's more in this than meets the eye. That machine is coming from the direction of Majorca. Franco has got a base there. By Jove, I wonder if it has anything to do with that old boy with the grey beard who came aboard at Gib!'

Algy looked at Biggles sharply. 'Why should it?'

'Because he's a Spaniard, or I've never seen one. He spoke in Spanish to the fellow who came to see him off.'

'You mean—?'

'Maybe I'm talking through my hat, but it just struck me that there might be something in it. What I mean is, maybe there is something or somebody on board this ship whom General Franco or the Catalonian Government doesn't want to reach port. A lot of ships have been bombed lately in these waters—even British ships.'

'You mean—you think this fellow might be going to *bomb* us?' cried Ginger aghast.

'Nothing he did would surprise me very much,' confessed Biggles. He raised his hand and pointed to the oncoming machine. 'One thing is certain,' he went on. 'He's making for this ship. It's a military machine, too—a two-seater. I can see the rear gun.'

Algy clutched Biggles' arm. 'You're right,' he said sharply. 'Those are bombs under his wings; they look like two hundred-and-thirty pounders—one on each side.'

They all started violently as a machine-gun started chattering somewhere in the fore part of the ship.

'What the devil!' cried Biggles angrily.

'Look out!' yelled Algy, as the aeroplane tilted its nose down in a steep dive, straight towards the ship.

Pandemonium brook loose in a din of shots, yells, and curses, but it was drowned in an ear-shattering volume of sound as the pilot of the machine opened up his engine. Its shadow flashed across the deck.

Biggles flung himself flat as a bomb detached itself from the port wing of the machine and hurtled downward. The others threw themselves beside him, their arms folded over their heads.

There was a moment of tense silence, broken only by the fast-diminishing roar of the aeroplane. Then the ship reeled and shuddered from stem to stern, as the bomb exploded somewhere amidships. There was a shrill hiss of escaping steam, and then a clatter as debris rained down on the deck.

11

Biggles was up in a moment, hurrying towards the spot where the bomb had exploded. Ginger would have passed him, but Biggles caught him by the arm and flung him back as a red-splashed scene of horror met his eyes.

'Watch out!' cried Algy tersely. 'Curse the fellow, he's coming back!' He pointed to the bomber, which was now banking steeply. Its nose swung down as it came in line with the ship, which had taken on a list that dragged it round in a wide curve.

Biggles' face turned pale; his lips set in a hard line, and he looked around with the sharp movements of a man who needs something urgently. His questing eyes came to rest on what they sought—the machine-gun which they had heard a moment or two earlier. He saw at a glance that it was a type unknown to him, but the spade grips and metal belt were familiar, and since the gun was already loaded he had no doubt about his ability to use it. 'Take what cover you can,' he snapped to the others, and vaulted over a splintered lifeboat to the gun. A member of the crew was half crouching, half lying, behind it, moaning feebly, his face buried in his hands. A thin trickle of blood oozed from between his fingers, and Biggles, investigating, found that the fellow's cheek had been gashed by a splinter. It was not a serious wound, so, with scant ceremony, Biggles dragged him aside and crouched behind the blue barrel of the gun. His fingers whitened as they took a holding*.

The aircraft was already within effective range, its

* When it is fired, a machine-gun jerks about violently, due to the recoil of the swiftly successive shots. In order to keep the barrel steady on the target it is necessary to drag on it with a good deal of force. This is called 'holding'.

nose tilted in a steep angle of dive. Above the roar of the engine came the wail of wind-torn wires and struts. The pilot was coming down straight over the stern of the vessel, offering what was, in effect, a sitting shot. That is to say, it was not necessary to move the barrel of the gun in order to keep the sights aligned.

Even as Biggles' thumbs pressed the double thumb-piece, he saw the bomb sail down from the wing of the attacking machine, but he continued to fire. Fifty rounds poured through the blue barrel in four seconds of time, but somewhat to Biggles' surprise the machine did not swerve an inch from its course. He knew that his shots were hitting the target, and only when the dive steepened suddenly did he realize what had happened. He had hit the pilot, who was no longer master of his machine. Simultaneously with this thought came the realization that the aeroplane would crash on the deck of its victim.

There was no time to do anything but dive for what cover was available. A swift rush across the now steeply sloping deck, and he flung himself behind the funnel. An instant later the decks heaved under him as the bomb exploded, and before the noise of falling debris had subsided came the splintering crash of the machine tearing through the rigging. The forward wireless mast was flung against the funnel, and while Biggles rolled clear of the flying splinters came the dull *whoosh* of exploding petrol.

Biggles, scrambling to his feet, saw that the deck was aflame with flowing petrol. 'Algy! Ginger!' he yelled.

The others came crawling from the hatch behind which they had taken cover.

'Lifebelts!' jerked out Biggles. 'This way. We've got about two minutes.'

Ignoring the captain and the surviving members of the crew, who were frantically trying to launch a lifeboat, he made his way to the lifebelt locker abaft the wrecked bridge. He passed a lifebelt to each of the others and proceeded to put on his own.

'What about a boat?' said Ginger.

'Look!' Biggles pointed to the crew. 'They'll never get that boat on the water. There! What did I tell you?' he said, as the bow of the boat swung down, throwing those who were already in it into the water. 'Come on, let's get clear. She'll roll over any moment now.'

As he spoke Biggles kicked off his shoes. The others did the same, and then, climbing over the rail, ran down the side of the heeling ship into the water.

'Keep together,' ordered Biggles as he struck out in a steady breast stroke away from the doomed vessel. Not until he was at what he considered a safe distance from it—for he was well aware of the vortex caused by a sinking ship, a vortex that would drag down everything that came within it—did he slow down. Turning, he looked at the stricken vessel.

It presented a terrible picture, a spectacle that none of them would ever forget. She was going down by the nose, her stern, with its twin propellers, being high in the air. Explosion followed explosion, mingled with the hiss of escaping steam. The entire deck, or that part of it that had not yet been submerged, was a sheet of flame. The petrol had even run down into the water, where it lapped against the iron sides of the ship as if impatient to conclude the work of destruction. Screams arose from the members of the crew who had been overtaken by the ever-spreading tide of burning spirit. Helpless, the three comrades could only watch.

'There she goes,' murmured Biggles.

The doomed ship slid forward like a great fish submerging. The waters closed over her, leaving nothing to show that she had ever been. All that remained was an area of what appeared to be burning water, a curious phenomenon on the blue sea.

'Well, ten minutes ago you were wanting something to happen,' remarked Algy quietly to Biggles. 'You've got your wish.'

'So it seems,' agreed Biggles evenly. 'But this, I need hardly say, is rather more than I bargained for. How far do you reckon we are from land?'

'Ten miles.'

'I should say rather less. There was a haze on the water.'

'Can we make it, do you think?' inquired Ginger.

'Lifebelts ought to keep us afloat for twenty-four hours. There is no tide in the Mediterranean, but if the current is favourable we ought to reach Spain. If it isn't, then it's no use. In that case our only chance is to be picked up by a ship. Our wireless operator might have had time to get out an SOS, but I doubt it. That first bomb hit somewhere near his cabin. Let's paddle towards the coast. Take it gently. It's no use exhausting ourselves.'

Chapter 2

A Swim in the Dark

For a long time they paddled on in silence, without apparently getting any nearer to the distant coast, which only showed as a faint blue shadow. It was difficult to tell, as Biggles pointed out to the others, at the same time expressing his appreciation of the fact that the sea was both calm and warm. The risk of succumbing to exposure was, therefore, greatly reduced.

Referring to their progress, he drew the others' attention to the fact that the distance of their horizon was now different from what it had been when they were on the ship, for then they were looking at it from an elevation of rather more than thirty feet. Another factor for which allowance had to be made was the westering sun; it was now on their left, whereas at noon it had been behind them. As evening was approaching, it was also a good deal lower in the sky.

With the coming of dusk the sea fell to a dead calm; not even a ripple stirred the surface. Not a boat of any description came within their restricted field of vision. They swam on quietly through a lonely sea, the only sound the gentle surging of the water around their bodies. Presently the distant shadows which they were hoping to reach merged with sea and sky, but with the closing in of night a lighthouse flashed an intermittent beam across the sky and gave them their direction.

Ginger cried aloud in alarm as a black body broke

the surface of the water near them; he gasped his relief when Biggles announced that it was only a harmless porpoise. They swam on into the deepening gloom. Pinpoints of light appeared in the distance.

After what seemed to Ginger to be an eternity of time, Biggles announced cheerfully that they were making progress. 'I think we've struck a favourable current,' he said. 'The lights are brighter than they were half an hour ago.'

'I can see one moving,' declared Algy. 'I think it's a car going along a road.'

'I think you're right,' agreed Biggles. 'Let's have a breather.'

They ceased swimming and floated in their lifebelts.

'How long have we been in the water?' asked Ginger.

'About six hours, for a guess. Has anybody got a watch? I left mine in the cabin.'

Algy and Ginger announced that they had done the same.

'Has anybody any money?' next inquired Biggles.

Algy announced that he had none at all. He had left all he had in the pocket of the slacks he had worn on the previous day. Ginger thought he had a pound in English money, and some change.

'Then we are going to have a rough passage home,' announced Biggles. 'I've only a pound or two, and a few hundred francs which I got for use in Marseilles. The rest of my money is in travellers' cheques, and I doubt if any one will cash them in Spain.'

'Let's get to Spain first. We'll get home all right if we do,' put in Algy.

'I think you're right,' returned Biggles, 'but unless we can get to the British Vice-Consul in Barcelona, or some other big town, it may not be so simple as you

17

seem to imagine. You haven't by any chance forgotten that Spain is in the throes of a civil war?'

'No, I haven't.'

'And you haven't overlooked the fact that in order to travel in a foreign country you need a passport? Have you got yours on you?'

'Gosh—no. It was in my suitcase.'

'So was mine—and so, I'll bet, was Ginger's. I thought of it on the ship, but I didn't feel like taking the risk of fetching it. Good thing I didn't; if I had I should have gone down with the ship. No matter. Don't let's worry about that now. Everything will turn out all right, although it would probably be easier if one of us could speak the language. I know only about a dozen words of Spanish. But let's push on. I don't think we've very far to go now.'

The reason for Biggles' optimism was obvious. The coast, or rather the innumerable lights that studded it, could be clearly seen. A little farther along, a maze of lights radiated from a common centre, and marked the position of what could only be a big city. It was soon apparent, too, that the current was carrying them along the coast towards it.

'If my geography is any good, judging by our position when the ship was struck, I should say that is either Tarragona or Barcelona,' said Biggles, referring, of course, to the city lights. 'I—well, I'm dashed! What do you make of that?'

'Fog,' replied Algy shortly.

The reason for Biggles' exclamation was an entirely unexpected development. The lights had disappeared. It was as if a curtain had been lowered between the swimmers and the shore.

'Yes, it must be fog. I can't think of anything else it

18

could be,' announced Biggles. 'Pity, just as we were so close. Never mind; it won't make any difference. The land will be there just the same when we get to it.'

They swam on.

'Fog, my grandmother!' cried Ginger sharply a moment later. 'Hark! Can you hear the aircraft? It's a big formation—bombers, I'll bet. It's a black-out. That's where the lights have gone.'

'Full marks to you, laddie,' answered Biggles. 'That's the answer all right. Looks as if we might be better off where we are than in the city.'

The low drone of the approaching aircraft drew nearer. A few moments later a shrill whistling, swiftly increasing in volume, almost drowned the noise of the engines.

Biggles laughed harshly. 'We've heard that noise before, haven't we, Algy?' he muttered.

'What is it?' asked Ginger.

'Bombs. Listen. They must be nearly on the carpet*.'

Hardly had the words left Biggles' lips when the sky was lit up by a blinding flash, followed quickly by others. A few seconds later came the reports, like thunderclaps, earth-shaking in their violence; even the surface of the sea was ruffled by the concussion.

'It looks as if we might have chosen a better spot to land,' remarked Algy grimly.

Before Biggles could answer another salvo of bombs rocked the city, the flashes of the explosions illuminating the sky like lightning. Red, leaping flames appeared in two places in the city.

'Dirty work,' said Biggles coldly.

* Slang: the ground

'It's all over, I think,' opined Algy. 'The machines are going back. Look at the archie*.'

Several anti-aircraft guns were firing at the raiders. The shells sparkled in the sky, but as far as they could see, to no useful purpose. The noise of the engines grew fainter, and it was clear that the raid was over. Lights began to appear again on the shore. They were now very close.

A minute or two later Biggles discovered that he could stand, and announced this welcome information with surprise. Presently, however, the reason was made manifest. A tongue of sand jutted out into the sea from a deserted foreshore.

Biggles, closely followed by the others, dragged himself wearily on to it. He took off his lifebelt, threw it on the sand, and sat down beside it. The others did the same.

'Well, we're on dry land, at any rate,' said Algy.

Biggles nodded. 'Yes,' he returned. 'The next thing is to find some dry clothes—or find a way of drying our own. If anybody else talks to me about sea trips he is going to hear something. We'd better keep on the move or our clothes will get cold, and so shall we. It's warmer in the water than out of it at this time of night. Are you both all right?'

On receiving assurance that they were, Biggles led the way up the beach, and after threading their way through some sand-dunes, they reached a road. It was little more than a track, and deserted, so they set off in the direction of the city.

'The first thing we had better look for is a boot shop,' decided Biggles presently. 'We can't go on walking

* Anti-aircraft gunfire

20

about in our socks. They look like houses in front of us, but I think we had better push right on. If we can pick up some shoes on the way, so well and good, but I think our best plan would be to go to an hotel where we can get some food and ask them to dry our clothes. We must try to get some pesetas, too.'

'Get some what?' inquired Ginger.

'Pesetas—Spanish money. It can't be more than half-past nine or ten, so we may find a change bureau open somewhere. There will probably be one at the railway station.'

Passing a number of more or less dilapidated dwellings, half an hour's walk brought them to the outskirts of the city proper. Beyond the fact that few people were about, there was nothing to show that the city had just been shaken by an air raid. The houses increased in size and importance as they walked on, and another ten minutes found them in a large open square, on one side of which sparkled the sea. The moon had risen and cast a gleaming track of light across the still water. Silhouetted against it rose a tall column, surmounted by a figure.

'We're in Barcelona,' announced Biggles. 'That's the famous statue of Christopher Columbus,' he added, indicating the column. 'He came here after discovering America. It's years since I was here, but if I remember right, the station is over there on the far side.'

The havoc caused by the bombs was now apparent. There were two yawning craters in the square itself, being regarded by a number of gesticulating men, mostly wearing berets on their heads. Skirting these, they climbed over a pile of fallen masonry and presently reached the station. As Biggles had hoped, they found a bureau open, where he changed three English pounds into Spanish currency. He had no idea of the rate of exchange, nor did he bother to inquire what it was. He simply laid the three notes on the small counter—sopping wet, of course. The cashier looked at them, and then at the vendor, suspiciously. A crafty smile that might have meant anything crossed his face, but after a close scrutiny of the notes he accepted them, and pushed a pile of peseta notes under the grille. Without troubling to count them, Biggles rolled them in a piece of paper which he tore from a nearby placard about air raids, and put them in his waistcoat pocket.

'No trouble about that,' he announced cheerfully as they retraced their steps to the square. 'All we need now is an hotel. There is bound to be one near the station. This street looks as good as any; we may as well try it.'

'Rambla de la Constit—something or other,' read Ginger from a label on the wall above a small but cosy-looking bar.

'There are a lot of troops about,' observed Algy, looking up the *rambla**.

'There's a war on,' returned Biggles dryly.

'There's a shoe shop,' cried Ginger, pointing to a dismal-looking hovel, outside which hung long lines of cheap-looking rope-soled sandals.

'They'll be better than nothing on our feet,' agreed Biggles. 'Let's get some.'

There was no question of explaining their needs to the owner of the shop, a little old man with a long grey beard and a pair of cheap glasses balanced on the end of his nose; he spoke no English, but Biggles simply pointed to his feet, and then at the sandals.

* Spanish: avenue

22

It needed little intelligence on the part of the old man to see what they wanted. He put a pile of shoes on the floor, and selected those which he knew from long experience would be about the right size.

In a few minutes the three had made their selection. Biggles paid the bill by the simple expedient of laying a hundred peseta note on the counter and picking up the change. Then they returned to the street.

'How about a cup of something hot—and one of those sandwich things?' suggested Ginger hopefully, nodding towards the bar-restaurant next door, in the window of which plates of various foods were displayed.

Biggles smiled. 'That's not a bad idea,' he admitted. 'I'm a bit peckish myself. Five minutes one way or another won't make much difference. We mustn't forget we've got to find the consulate, to get some sort of identity papers, or we may land ourselves into trouble.'

Ginger led the way to the entrance. Over the door, on a cheap scroll, was written what was presumably the name of the bar-restaurant. '*Casa Reposada*,' he read aloud. 'What does that mean?'

'Home of quiet—or, more literally, home of repose,' returned Biggles. 'Go ahead.'

They entered. There was nothing to indicate that the trouble Biggles feared was waiting for them inside.

Chapter 3
A Dangerous Mission

Indeed, at first glance the bar appeared to be singularly well named. It was, in fact, unexpectedly restful, the only sound coming from a radio that stood on the counter transmitting a popular opera, to which the barman, leaning over the counter with his chin cupped in the palms of his hands, listened in rapt attention.

The room was small and typical of its kind. Posters announcing national lotteries with huge prizes, and bullfights, decorated the walls, and more than half concealed the faded wallpaper. A low bench ran completely round the room; and conveniently placed were a number of round, marble-topped tables. The floor was thickly sprinkled with sawdust, and equipped with the inevitable spittoons, for the accommodation of patrons in a land where the habit of spitting is not regarded as a breach of good manners. Behind the barman, on shelves, stood many rows of bottles, often bearing flamboyant labels.

There was only one customer present, a rather stout, sallow-faced man, who looked up sharply from the newspaper he was reading, and subjected the new arrivals to a close scrutiny as they passed his table. Biggles met his eyes squarely, and nodded a perfunctory greeting, whereupon the man reverted to his original reclining position on the bench, and buried his face behind the newspaper.

Biggles chose a table a short distance farther along,

24

and sank down on the bench with a sigh of relief. 'I vote for big cups of hot chocolate,' he said as the others sat down, one on either side of him. 'It's one of the things they make well in Spain.' Then aloud to the bar-keeper, '*Hi! señor. Tres chocolate!*'

The bar-keeper rose slowly from his position on the counter and, turning the radio higher—presumably so that he would still be able to hear it—disappeared through a door into the back regions.

Biggles frowned his disapproval as the shrill voice of a soprano came over the wireless instrument. 'I hope she isn't going to keep that up,' he muttered. 'That noise would give a corpse a headache.'

At that moment the door opened and a repulsive-looking hunchback came in. His lips parted in what he may have thought was a smile, but what to Ginger seemed a very unpleasant leer. His dark eyes flashed round the room; they rested for a moment on the man behind the newspaper, and then settling on the three strangers, he advanced towards them, brandishing in his right hand a small book.

'What does he want, do you suppose?' inquired Ginger.

'He's selling lottery tickets,' answered Biggles. He had to shout to make himself heard above the noise of the radio. 'You can never get away from that in Spain. It is said that one half of the country lives by selling lottery tickets, and the other half spend their time listening to the results on the wireless.' He waved to the hunchback to go away, but the man persisted in his unwelcome attention until the situation became embarrassing. Fortunately at this moment the bar-keeper returned with the drinks, and seeing that his customers were being disturbed with what sounded like a violent stream of invective, drove the hunchback away from them.

With an evil scowl the ticket-vendor retired, and breathing noisily, as if asthma or some other lung trouble added to his other misfortunes, transferred his attentions to the other customer.

There was a rattle of cups and saucers as the bar-keeper set them on the marble table. This done, he returned to the counter where, after turning down the wireless, he took up his original position of keen appreciation of the music.

'That's better,' mused Biggles. 'I found that lady a bit trying.'

Ginger noticed that the hunchback had gone. 'I'm glad that creature has pushed off, too,' he said quietly. 'He gave me the horrors.'

Nothing more was said for a few minutes as the airmen busied themselves pouring out and drinking their chocolate, which was all that Biggles had hoped it would be. 'We had better be moving on,' he said at last, and was about to call for his bill when the door opened and another visitor entered. From the unmistakable London cut of his clothes he appeared to be English, and Biggles, after a quick start of surprise, turned to Algy.

'If that isn't Dicky Frazer I'll eat my shirt,' he said quietly. 'You remember Dicky, Algy; he was on the Headquarters Intelligence staff during the war*. We met him once or twice with Major Raymond.'

Algy looked hard at the newcomer who, without a sign of recognition, although his eyes had rested on

*First World War 1914–1918

them for a moment, walked to the far side of the room and sat down on the bench.

'You may be right,' answered Algy in a low voice, for the man under discussion was not more than twelve feet away. 'His face is vaguely familiar, but I didn't see Frazer often enough to be able to swear to him after all this time. It's easy enough to find out, though. Why not speak to him?'

Biggles, without moving, addressed the man whom he thought he recognized. 'Pardon me,' he said, 'but aren't you the Frazer I knew in the R.F.C. during the war? Remember me—Bigglesworth? I met you, I believe, with Major Raymond.'

The man looked up, face impassive. 'I'm afraid you're making a mistake,' he answered unsmilingly. 'My name is not Frazer. I know no one of that name, and to the best of knowledge I have never seen you before in my life.' With that the man settled back, his eyes on the door as if he was expecting some one.

Biggles looked at the others, a blank expression on his face. For a moment he did not speak, while his expression changed slowly to one of hard conviction. 'That man is a liar,' he said in a curious voice, under his breath. 'His name *is* Frazer. I'd stake my life on it. I recognized his voice the moment he opened his mouth. What's the big idea, I wonder? In any case he is British, and you'd think in a place like this he'd be only too glad to pass the time of day with fellow countrymen. Not that it matters two hoots. If he wants to mind his own business, it's none of ours.'

Nobody spoke while Biggles felt in his pocket for money with which to pay the bill. The wireless concert concluded with a burst of applause from the unseen audience, and the bar-keeper switched off.

27

The almost tense silence—for so it seemed after the music—was broken by two sounds. From somewhere just outside the door came a wheezing asthmatical cough, and, nearer at hand, a soft drip, drip, drip, as though a pipe was leaking. Biggles lifted up the chocolate jug, thinking it might be cracked. He did it inconsequentially, with an air of casual curiosity. He made no comment, however. Instead, Ginger spoke.

'That confounded hunchback is still hanging about outside,' he said. 'Waiting for us to come out, I expect. Got his pals with him, too, by the look of it.'

Biggles glanced towards the door, beyond which two or three shadowy figures could just be seen. Then, for no reason that he was aware of, his eyes went back to the man whom he had thought was Frazer. Instinctively he stiffened at the expression on his face. The man was not looking at him. His eyes were riveted on the floor near the feet of the other solitary occupant of the bar, he who had been reading the newspaper. So tense was his expression that Biggles looked to see what he was staring at, and he, too, stared spellbound at what he saw.

He recovered himself quickly, however. 'Stand by,' he almost hissed. 'Something funny has been happening here.'

The others looked down. Nobody spoke. Comment was unnecessary. The dark crimson pool in which the newspaper-reader's feet rested could be only one thing. From the same spot came the ominous drip—drip—drip.

Biggles started to move, but the man who had denied that his name was Frazer frustrated him. Four swift paces and he had crossed the room. With a quick movement he moved the newspaper so that the man's face could be seen.

Ginger had a momentary view of staring eyes and a sagging jaw. Then the newspaper was moved back to its original position, covering the face. The man who had made the investigation returned to his seat.

Biggles glanced at the bar-keeper, and saw that he was making up his accounts in a small book. It was obvious that he had noticed nothing amiss.

Biggles addressed the others in a voice that was low yet vibrant. 'We'd better get out of this,' he said.

'Bigglesworth!'

Biggles, who had half-risen in his seat, stiffened. His eyes flashed to the man who had spoken. It was the Britisher.

'Sit down.'

There was something so authoritative in the tense voice that Biggles instinctively complied.

'Sit down and sit still.'

Biggles nodded acquiescence.

'Don't move and don't speak,' came the voice again. 'Behave naturally—as if you're still drinking. But listen!'

Biggles glanced at the man who was speaking. He had taken a cigarette from his case and was now lighting it with an air of complete nonchalance. Only his voice betrayed the true atmosphere of the situation.

'Don't look at me,' came the voice again, low but tense. 'You were right,' it continued. 'I'm Frazer. I'm still on the same job—understand? I'm in a jam. So are you. If the people outside saw you speaking to me just now, you'll never get out of here alive—none of you. I'm not being dramatic—but it's as bad as that.

I've got something in my pocket, a paper, that has got to reach the Foreign Office. It's *got* to. The dead man near you was my messenger. He was waiting for me here. My plans have gone wrong. They've got him. Now they'll get me. Have you seen a hunchback?'

'Yes.'

'Ah! Then there will be a score of men waiting outside. They'll be all round. Goudini—that's the hunchback—is thorough. I can't get through—they'll see to that. It doesn't matter about me, but the paper has got to go. It may mean life or death to the Empire. It's as important as that. I want you to take it. There is just a chance that they have not associated you with me. Will you take it?'

'Of course.'

'Good! Be careful; they're watching us now through the windows. Do exactly what I tell you. I'm going to put an envelope on the floor and kick it as near to you as I can. When you go out, drop something; pick up whatever you drop, and the envelope at the same time. Then go. Don't go the front way. On the right-hand side of the bar there is a door marked *caballeros*.* It's the lavatory. Go straight down the corridor which you will see in front of you. It leads to the kitchen. On the far side of the kitchen you'll see the back door. Get out that way. They'll be watching it, but you may get through. I couldn't. It would be hopeless. Don't move yet. I'm going out of the front door. They'll rush me then. That's your chance to go out the back way. Got that?'

'Quite clear.'

*Spanish: Gentlemen

'Good! But don't think I'm exaggerating. My chances of getting out of here alive are about one in a hundred. Yours are one in ten. They'll kill you without the slightest compunction if they think you're with me. I don't know what you're doing here, but it doesn't matter. Make for London. If you get there, tell them what happened.'

From outside came again the wheezing cough.

'That's Goudini,' said Frazer.

Ginger stole a glance at the man whom by this time he realized was a British Secret Service agent. There was nothing in his manner now to show that anything unusual was happening. He was leaning back, smoking a cigarette contentedly, his eyes on the ceiling.

'All set?' he inquired casually.

'All set,' returned Biggles softly. Then to the others, 'You've heard what has been said. Stand by.'

'Here comes the letter,' said Frazer, and took out his cigarette case. There was a clang of metal as he dropped it on the floor. Several cigarettes fell out. His foot jerked, and a small manilla-coloured envelope skimmed across the sawdust. Then he picked up the loose cigarettes, and laying his case open on the table, proceeded to put the cigarettes back into it.

Biggles' foot was already resting on the envelope. He took out a hundred-peseta note and laid it on the table; then he coughed, and the slight draught carried it to the floor. Stooping, he picked it up, and the envelope with it. Then he walked slowly up to the bar and paid his bill.

Frazer was also on his feet, moving slowly towards the door. 'Cheerio,' he said quietly.

'Cheerio,' answered Biggles, and turned to the *lavabo.**

The others followed close behind.

Chapter 4
Unexpected Developments

As the door swung to behind them Biggles whirled round on the others. 'Trust us to walk into something like this,' he said grimly. 'Still, there it is. You know what we've got to do. The letter comes first. It's in my breast pocket. If anything happens to me, get the letter at any cost and go on with it. That's all. Come on.'

As Frazer had said, a narrow corridor appeared in front of them, and down this Biggles strode. Before he had reached the door which faced them at the end, however, there came the crash of a pistol shot, followed by two more in swift succession. Biggles did not stop. 'I reckon they've got Frazer,' he said simply, and pushed open the door.

An old woman looked over her shoulder from a pan in which she was cooking something, and greeted them with a stream of Spanish. Biggles took no notice, but crossing the kitchen, heavy with the smell of garlic, he opened the door on the far side, and looked out. The narrow street into which it opened appeared to be deserted, but two shadows that faded quickly into a doorway gave the lie to this illusion.

'They're outside, waiting,' he flung over his shoulder to the others. 'Oh, be quiet, woman,' he said angrily to the old dame who was still assailing them with what sounded like a stream of protest. 'Come on,' he said quickly to the others. 'We shall have to put a bold front on it, and try to bluff our way through. We can't stay here.' With that, he stepped out into the street, the others at his heels. The old woman slammed the door behind them.

Biggles was not in the least concerned with the old woman. He was far more anxious about the three men who appeared suddenly in the road about ten yards farther along. Looking the other way, he gave an exclamation of warning as two more men stepped out of a doorway and hurried towards them. 'Looks as if we're in for a rough house,' he said quietly.

Ginger, conscious of a feeling of helplessness, looked about for a weapon, even if it were only a stone. But there was nothing. 'Let's rush 'em,' he suggested crisply.

Biggles hesitated, as well he might. Had he been able to speak Spanish he would have felt better equipped for what he knew was coming, and in his impotence he muttered something to that effect. 'Take it quietly until they show their hand,' he ordered, and took a pace towards the men now closing in on them.

At that moment a new and unexpected development occurred. A saloon motor-car swung round a corner about fifty yards away, and with a screech of its electric horn, bore down on the men in a manner which at once made it clear that if they did not get out of the way the driver would run over them.

It did not cross Biggles' mind that the car was associated with their own affair. There was little or no reason why it should. He, like the men in front of him, stepped back against the wall of the nearest house, for in the narrow street there was little margin of safety. He was not a little astounded, therefore, when he saw the door of the car swing open, although the car did not stop. He was completely taken aback when, as the car drew level, a voice yelled, in English, 'Get in!' That was all, but the desperate urgency in the speaker's tone of voice said volumes.

Biggles did not hesitate. He realized that he might be stepping into a trap, but there was no time for consideration. No situation could have been more dangerous than the one they were already in, so he jumped, literally, at the opportunity offered for escape. Being nearest, he flung open the rear door for the others before diving into the seat beside the driver. Algy and Ginger flung themselves pell-mell into the back seat— no easy matter, for the car had started to accelerate the moment Biggles was inside it. They fell in a heap on the floor, which may have been just as well, for several shots rang out. There was a crash of glass and splintering woodwork.

A man grabbed at the front door, which was still swinging open, but Biggles' foot shot out, and catching the man in the stomach, sent him flying. Yells mingled with more shots. There was a hiss of escaping air and a wheel bumped crazily on its rim, but the driver did not stop. Still on the floor, Algy tried to reach the rear door to close it, but with a fearful crash it struck a lamp-post, and he nearly lost his fingers as the door came to with a bang that shattered the window. Then the car swung into a broad, well-lighted thoroughfare, and in a moment the scene was changed.

Biggles managed to reach the door beside him and close it. Then, for the first time, he looked at the man who had rescued them, and who was gazing ahead with a fixed expression as he picked his way through the traffic.

His serenity told Biggles nothing beyond the fact that he was middle-aged, and clearly a foreigner, although to what nationality he belonged he could not even guess. He was well-dressed in a dark suit, and wore a black Homburg hat above what was undoubtedly a good-looking face. A carefully trimmed black moustache adorned his upper lip. But still he did not speak, nor did he, in fact, take the slightest notice of the men whom he had picked up in such alarming circumstances. They might not have been there for all the attention he gave them.

Biggles opened the conversation—or rather, he tried to. 'Thanks,' he said. 'You arrived at what I believe is known as the crucial moment.'

'Don't mention it,' replied the man without taking his eyes off the road. His English was perfect, but there was just a suspicion of accent which told Biggles that he had not been mistaken in his opinion that the man was a foreigner.

'How did you know we were in a jam?' inquired Biggles, really in the hope of finding out something about the man and the new circumstances in which they now found themselves.

'It's my business to know,' was all the answer he got.

Biggles shrugged his shoulders at this uncompromising announcement. 'Where are we bound for?' he next inquired.

'You'll see.'

After that Biggles gave it up. It was clear that their benefactor did not intend to talk.

'You all right in the back?' Biggles asked, looking over his shoulder.

'Very comfortable, thank you,' replied Algy, who, with Ginger, was now sitting on the seat. 'You might ask the gentleman next to you how far he is going,' he went on. 'You might point out to him, too, that our clothes are wet and we should very much like to dry them.'

'The gentleman in front does not appear to be very communicative,' replied Biggles gravely, with a faint suspicion of sarcasm in his voice. 'He has no doubt decided where he is going to take us.'

If the driver noticed the sarcasm he gave no indication of it. He drove on, not very fast on account of the punctured tyre, picking his way carefully through pedestrians, who were chiefly soldiers and girls, and other traffic. Several times he had almost to stop as he rounded bomb craters, or piles of fallen brickwork and other debris. Presently, however, he turned out of the boulevard into what was clearly a residential quarter of the city, for tall, well-built houses could be seen through a leafy screen of oleander trees that formed an avenue. An occasional palm reared its graceful fronds from the front garden of a house.

They passed through several similar avenues, and after a drive lasting about twenty minutes the car approached another well-lighted *rambla* along which a stream of traffic was passing. There was surprisingly little to show that the country was in the throes of civil war, was the thought passing through Biggles' mind as the car pulled up in front of the portico of what appeared to be a large private hotel.

The driver opened the window and looked round carefully before opening the door and stepping out. 'Come on,' he said in a peremptory voice.

'You know where we are—I don't,' murmured Biggles as he followed him on to the pavement.

The others got out and followed their mysterious driver who, after a nod to a uniformed porter, entered the hotel, leaving the car where it stood. They crossed a small palm lounge and came to a halt before an elevator.

Biggles was rather in a quandary. He was by no means happy at thus blindly following a man whom he did not know, nor did he intend doing so much longer without some sort of explanation. But in the circumstances he felt that, as the man had undoubtedly rescued them from a very serious predicament, he could not very well be churlish. As he reasoned it out, too, he felt that the man must be a friend or he would not have taken the risks he had, risks that had involved the partial destruction of an expensive motor-car.

Nevertheless, while they were waiting for the lift, Biggles took the opportunity of pressing his inquiries a little closer. 'Look here,' he said quietly, addressing the stranger, 'this is all very well, but what's the idea? Naturally, we are very much obliged to you for getting us out of a scrape, but even so we have some right to know just who and what you are—that is, if you expect us to take orders from you.'

'You'll understand when we get upstairs,' answered the man shortly.

'Well, having come so far we may as well go the rest of the way, since we appear to be near the end of the journey,' returned Biggles.

At that moment the lift appeared. Without speaking, they all got into it. Biggles noticed that it stopped at the fourth floor.

The stranger led the way for a short distance down a corridor; then, taking a key from his pocket, he opened a door and, switching on the electric light, invited the others to enter.

Biggles glanced around swiftly. There was nobody

38

in the room, which was comfortably furnished as a bed-sitting room, so he walked in. The others followed and stood beside him.

The stranger closed the door quietly and then turned an expressionless face to the three airmen. He put his hand in his pocket, and before a suspicion of his intention crossed their minds, they found themselves staring blankly into the muzzle of an automatic pistol.

The stranger fixed a pair of unsmiling eyes on Biggles' face. 'Give me that envelope,' he said.

Chapter 5
Goudini Again

Silence followed this unexpected order.

Biggles was as much taken aback as the others. Whatever he had expected—and he was prepared for almost anything—it was certainly not this. He could not reconcile it with the mysterious stranger's previous actions. In fact, he had not even considered the possibility of the man knowing that he had the document. How *did* he know? he asked himself, for Frazer had passed the envelope so adroitly that nobody except he and those to whom he had passed it could have been aware of the transaction. It was impossible that Frazer had told the man what he was going to do before he entered the *Casa Reposada*, because he, Frazer, judging by his subsequent actions, did not know that Biggles was in Barcelona until he saw him in the bar. Once inside the room, he had not left it until he had departed for the last time. Biggles took into account the possibility of Frazer surviving long enough after he had been shot—if, indeed, he had been shot—to pass the information on, but the chances against this were so remote that they were barely worth consideration.

'Come on; pass it over,' said the man again impatiently.

But Biggles was not prepared to capitulate so readily, or even to admit that he had the document. 'Envelope?' he questioned, putting on a blank look. 'What do you mean—envelope?'

'I saw Frazer kick it across the floor to you,' was the cool reply.

This ready answer shook even Biggles' composure, but it explained much. He perceived that if the man had actually witnessed the transfer of the envelope, and this was no longer in doubt, further denial would serve no useful purpose. 'I see,' he said softly. 'Where were you?'

'Where I could see, of course,' was the evasive answer. 'I didn't trail Frazer all the way from Rome to Barcelona to lose sight of him at the end of it.'

'Are you a friend or an enemy?' asked Biggles wonderingly, for there was still much that he did not understand.

'Neither—or both, whichever suits my book,' was the curious reply, spoken curtly.

Biggles nodded gently. 'You—work for yourself?'

'It's time you knew that, if you're in the business.'

Biggles smiled faintly. 'That's just it. I'm not in the business,' he said quietly.

'From the way you acted tonight it doesn't look that way to me.'

'Maybe not, but it's true.'

'How did you come into this?'

'By accident,' admitted Biggles frankly.

'Some people might believe that—but not me,' sneered the other. 'Try it on Goudini and see how it works. He'll be combing the city for us by this time. But come on, we've stood here talking long enough. I don't want to shoot you unless you make me, but I've got to get away, and when I go I'm taking the paper with me. Pass it over!' The stranger jerked up the muzzle of his weapon threateningly.

Biggles could see no alternative but to comply. That

the man knew that he had the letter was certain. To resist would mean that they would probably all lose their lives to no purpose, for the man would take the letter, anyway. So, reluctantly, he put his hand in his pocket.

At that moment the light went out.

The stranger choked a curse. Then his voice came from somewhere near the door. 'Keep still!' he snapped viciously. 'If I hear a sound I shall fire at it.'

Before the man had finished speaking, Biggles, from the crouching position on the floor to which he had dropped the instant the light went out, guessed the reason for the sudden darkness.

From outside came the distant wail of sirens, and, nearer at hand, shouts of alarm and warning. A steady drone of aero engines became audible. General Franco's bombers were making another raid.

It was an extraordinary situation. Biggles, realizing the folly of such a move, had no intention of trying to reach the man, whom he could visualize standing with his back to the door and his finger on the trigger of the pistol, for to do so without being heard was out of the question. Movement in that direction would, he knew, invite disaster, for there was no doubt in his mind that the stranger would shoot on the slightest provocation. Yet he felt that this providential opportunity to do something should not be allowed to pass without an attempt being made to take advantage of it. As he entered the room he had noticed a door on the left-hand side of it. It was not, he thought, a sitting-room, or the room in which he now crouched would not have been furnished as it was. Nor did he think that it could be another exit to the corridor. He suspected that it was either a large wardrobe cupboard or a bathroom. He decided to find out.

But at his first movement the stranger's voice came warningly. 'Keep still!'

Biggles obeyed. It was, he found, impossible to move without making some slight sound, so to persist would be only to court trouble. If the stranger started to shoot he could hardly fail to hit somebody.

For a minute or two silence reigned, a silence broken only by the steady drone of the bombers, increasing in volume as the machines approached their objective. Biggles was not unprepared for what happened next. The roar of the first salvo of bombs, not far away, followed immediately by the rumble of falling brick-work, gave him an opportunity which he was not slow to seize, for the terrifying noises outside would effectually drown any sound that he was likely to make in a stealthy passage across the room. More bombs fell, and by the time the noise of the explosions had died away he had reached the doorway, after colliding with some-body—either Algy or Ginger, he did not know which—on the way.

But if the stranger did not actually hear the move-ment he evidently suspected it, for the pistol spat, bringing down a small shower of plaster from the ceil-ing. The flash revealed the whereabouts of every one in the room. The stranger, seeing his suspicions con-firmed, fired again; but Biggles, knowing that the shot would come, had flung open the door and thrown him-self inside. As he flattened himself against the wall another bullet struck the doorpost.

From the faint moonlight that entered the window—for, unlike those in the other room, the blind and cur-tains had not been drawn—Biggles saw that he was

43

in a bathroom. He noticed, too, as is customary in bathrooms, that the key was on the inside of the door, so he lost no time in turning it. A stride took him to the window, but a glance was sufficient to show him that there was no escape that way. It was a forty-foot drop into a yard, with some waste land beyond.

For a moment or two he stood still, thinking quickly.

In the other room, Ginger, with whom Biggles had collided on his way to the bathroom, lay on the floor and wondered what was going to happen next. He had assumed the prone position because, with bullets flying, and more likely to fly, it seemed to him—as indeed it was—the safest place.

'Keep still, you two,' snarled the stranger, obviously put out by the success of Biggles' manoeuvre.

'All right, I'm not moving,' answered Ginger. 'I've nothing to move for, anyway,' he added simply, with a sincerity that was obviously genuine.

A trumpet sounded in the street below, and a minute later the light came on, making the man with the pistol once more master of the situation. He ordered Algy and Ginger to get on their feet, put their hands up and stand against the wall; and they had no choice but to comply. Then, keeping them covered, he advanced cautiously to the bathroom door. Holding the pistol in his right hand, he tried the handle of the door with the other, but it was, as we know, locked on the inside.

'Open this door, curse you!' he demanded furiously.

To Ginger's utter amazement, the door swung open, to disclose a curious spectacle. Biggles was standing by the bathroom window, which was wide open. His right arm projected through it into the air. In his hand he held the fateful manilla envelope.

'Shoot me, and away goes the letter,' announced Biggles, cheerfully.

For a moment the man's impotent anger was such that it seemed as if he might shoot, whatever the consequences might be. But evidently he thought better of it. With the pistol covering Biggles from a range of not more than two yards, he could only stand and glare.

'Well?' inquired Biggles coolly. 'What are you going to do about it? Do we stand here until one of us dies of starvation?'

'Give me that letter,' ground out the man through clenched teeth.

'No,' smiled Biggles. 'There is a porter down in the yard. I'd rather give it to him.' He looked down into the yard. 'Hi!' he called, '*guarda—comprendo**?' So saying, he tossed the letter into space. 'How do you like my Spanish?' he inquired as he turned back into the room.

Again it looked as if the man might shoot him in his anger, but he did not. He flashed a glance at the other two, still standing against the wall, and then backed swiftly towards the door. 'You try to follow me and you'll get what's coming to you,' he snapped, and slipping out of the door, locked it behind him.

Biggles joined the others in the bedroom. 'Well, that's that,' he said cheerfully. 'But let's get busy; we've no time to lose.'

'But the letter?' gasped Ginger.

'It's in my pocket; it was only the envelope I dropped,' replied Biggles, quietly. 'Unfortunately, he'll find that out as soon as he gets hold of it, so we'd better be doing something.'

* Spanish: keep—understand?

As he spoke he crossed over to the window, and dragging one of the curtains aside, discovered that it overlooked the avenue and the front entrance to the hotel.

'What are you going to do?' asked Algy. 'What the dickens can we do, anyway? We are locked in.'

'I know that, but we've got to find a way out somehow,' returned Biggles tersely. 'That door looks pretty heavy, and I doubt if we shall be able to force it—at any rate, not without making such a row that the hotel staff will come up to see what's going on. We don't want to bring the manager up; we might find it awkward to explain what we're doing here. In the meantime, our friend with the pistol, having discovered how he has been tricked, will soon be back looking—Great Scott! There he is now, down there by the door. Who is he talking to? I believe it's—yes, it is. It's the porter who picked up the envelope.'

'There was actually a porter down there then?' inquired Algy.

'There certainly was,' replied Biggles. 'It was seeing him that gave me the idea.'

While this conversation had been going on the others had joined Biggles at the window and saw that what he had said was true. Their recent acquaintance was engaged in conversation with a porter on the pavement. Some money changed hands, and the watchers could hardly believe their good fortune when the unknown man put the envelope in his pocket with barely a glance at it. He seemed anxious to be gone, and the reason for his apprehension was soon apparent.

He had hurried to his car, which was still standing at the edge of the kerb, and had actually reached the door when another car came swerving round the corner. The brakes wailed, and even before the second car had stopped a man had jumped out, followed immediately by another. There was no doubt as to their objective.

The man standing at the door of the stationary car seemed suddenly to become alive to his danger. His hand flashed to his pocket, but he was too late. A revolver roared, and he staggered, still clinging to the door of the car. Again came the bark of a revolver, and this time there was no mistake. The possessor of the envelope collapsed on the pavement, his automatic falling from his nerveless fingers.

'Good heavens, it's Goudini!' cried Ginger in a hoarse voice.

It was true. The hunchback had got out of the car, and while the others stood on guard, he hobbled over to the fallen man. Kneeling beside him, his hand went swiftly through his pockets. The envelope came to light. He examined it closely, thrusting his fingers under the flap. Then he looked up at the windows of the hotel, all of which could be seen clearly in the light of the lamp over the hotel door.

Biggles stepped back quickly, dragging the others with him. 'There's no fooling *him*, I'm afraid,' he exclaimed bitterly. 'It looks as though we aren't out of the wood yet—not by a long way. I'd sooner deal with the fellow who was up here just now than with that dreadful-looking piece of work.'

'That lottery ticket business is only a blind, I suppose,' muttered Ginger.

'Of course. He killed Frazer's messenger by stabbing him. The noise of the wireless prevented us from hearing anything. It all happened just as we were pouring out our chocolate; when he left us he went over to the fellow who was reading the newspaper—you remember?' As Biggles finished speaking he took a surreptitious peep round the corner of the blind.

'I wonder who he is?' murmured Algy.

'We're likely to know soon enough. He has just come into the hotel,' announced Biggles grimly.

Chapter 6
A Difficult Situation

Algy lit a cigarette which he took from a half-empty packet on the mantelpiece, and flicked the dead match into the grate with a gesture of resignation. 'Trust us to choose the one bar in Barcelona where there was trouble brewing,' he said with bitter sarcasm. 'Barcelona—where the nuts come from. We're not nuts, we're mutts.'

'Never mind about that,' answered Biggles shortly. 'We'd better be doing something.'

'Go ahead,' invited Algy.

'I'm going to get rid of this letter for a start,' declared Biggles.

'Rid of it? What's it about, anyway?'

Biggles took the letter from his pocket, and unfolding it, discovered that it was a single sheet of paper. He looked down at it curiously. One glance was enough. 'It's in code,' he said. 'I suppose we ought to have been prepared for that. One thing is certain—this chap Goudini mustn't get hold of it. He was Frazer's biggest fear. What's the alternative? We don't want to call the police into this, although it wouldn't surprise me if they came in on their own account, considering that we've been associated with two murders. If they find this document on us we shall all be for the high jump, make no mistake about that. In a city seething with spies, foreigners carrying code messages are likely to get short shrift, and you can't blame the Barcelona government for that. That's why I say we've got to get rid of it.'

'You mean you'll hide it—in this room?'

'If I know anything about Mr. Goudini, he'll soon be stripping the paper off the walls looking for it. No, it's no use leaving it here.' Biggles paced the floor deep in thought. 'There's only one thing to do,' he decided at last. 'It's a big risk, but then so is anything else we might do.'

The others watched with intense curiosity as he proceeded to put his plan into action. From the mantelpiece he took a small, cheap china image about four inches high. Folding the letter into the smallest possible compass, he pushed it through a small hole in the base. Then from the fire-place he took a piece of newspaper, discoloured with age, that had been arranged behind the bars to conceal the empty grate. This he rolled round the image in the form of a loose ball. 'Come and watch where this falls,' he said, and led the way to the bathroom window.

He peered out. Below lay a yard. Not a soul was in sight. Beyond the yard, and adjacent to it, was a piece of waste land which, judging by its appearance, had been used for a long time as an unofficial rubbish-tip.

'What on earth are you going to do?' asked Ginger in alarm.

'Watch,' Biggles told him, and hurled the paper ball, with its precious contents, far out beyond the yard.

It landed on the rubbish dump, bounced, rolled a little, and came to rest.

'I can see it,' said Ginger.

'I think we can all see it,' murmured Biggles. 'If we can keep together, so well and good. If for any reason we get split up, any one who gets clear will have to

50

make for this spot, collect the paper, and try to get it through to Whitehall. And while I think of it, you'd both better have some money in case of accidents. All I have would not be enough to get any one of us back home, I'm afraid, but a little is better than nothing.'

As he spoke Biggles took out his wad of notes and divided the money between the three of them. 'Now let us see if we can do anything about this door,' he suggested when they had put the money in their pockets.

They returned to the bedroom, but before they could reach the door there was a confused murmur of voices outside, followed quickly by a peremptory knock.

'*Entrar**,' called Biggles at once. 'That is, if you can,' he added under his breath.

The handle of the door turned, and it creaked as a force was applied to it, but the door remained closed. There was an exclamation of irritation outside, and another knock.

'*Entrar!*' called Biggles again.

The noise of some one attempting to open the door was repeated. Then a voice spoke sharply in Spanish.

'*No comprendo***,' called Biggles. 'English–*Ingles*.' He turned to the others. 'This is an awful nuisance, not being able to speak the language properly,' he muttered impatiently.

'Open the door,' ordered a voice outside, in English but with a strong foreign accent.

'I can't. We are locked in. The man took the key,' replied Biggles to the unknown speaker, although he thought he recognized the voice. 'I think it's friend Goudini,' he whispered.

---

* Spanish: come in
** Spanish: I don't understand

Came another murmur of voices outside. There was a delay of two or three minutes, during which time the silence was broken only by a loose, wheezing cough, which confirmed what Biggles already suspected. Then a key was inserted in the lock, and the door opened abruptly. The hunchback stood in the doorway. Behind him were five black-coated men. Two wore black Homburg hats; two wore berets. The other, hatless, was clearly the hotel manager, or secretary.

The hunchback's eyes darted round the room as he advanced. They came to rest on Biggles. He held out his hand. 'Give it to me,' he demanded.

Biggles, of course, knew well enough what he meant. 'Give you what?' he asked blankly.

'The paper.'

Biggles raised his eyebrows. 'What are you talking about?' he said. 'What paper do you mean?'

Goudini walked to the bed and sat down on the edge of it. The other men remained just inside the doorway. His dark, piercing eyes regarded Biggles steadily, but a faint curiosity came into them. 'Who are you?' he asked.

'I might ask you the same question,' returned Biggles lightly.

'Zat is no secret in Barcelona,' was the prompt and unexpected reply. 'I am Juan Goudini, Deputy Commissar Special of Intelligence and Propaganda. Now, who are you? Speak.'

Biggles stared at the Spaniard, not a little startled by this information. It had not occurred to him that Goudini might be an important official of the Barcelona Government, so the announcement came as a complete surprise, leaving him uncertain whether he was glad or sorry. But he answered frankly.

'In that case I must, of course, answer your question,' he said readily. 'Although it will convey nothing to you, I may say that my name is Bigglesworth. These are my friends. This morning we were on a ship, on a convalescent cruise. The ship was bombed by an aeroplane which appeared to come from the direction of Majorca. The ship sank, and we were thrown into the water, and we were fortunate enough to be able to reach the shore not far from this city. Having no Spanish money, we went to the station bureau and changed some English pounds into pesetas. The man will no doubt remember us because the notes were wet. They were wet, and we were wet because we had just come out of the sea. It was our intention to report to the British Consulate, but having no shoes, we bought those we now wear. Next door was a bar. Feeling cold and tired, we went in for a drink. I think I am right in saying that you saw us there. As we were about to leave we discovered that a man had been stabbed to death. Fearing that we, strangers and without passports, might be involved in this, we tried to leave the bar—foolishly, perhaps—by the back door. As we did so we were attacked by unknown men. A motorcar came up the street. The driver invited us to enter. Naturally, in the circumstances we did so. He brought us here. In this room he spoke of a paper. I answered him as I answered you, whereupon he went out and locked us in. That was about ten minutes ago. Through this window we saw the man prepare to enter his automobile. He was shot. We were still thinking of how we could get out when you came.'

Biggles felt—and hoped—that his story sounded plausible, but he was well aware that there were weak

53

spots in it. He feared Goudini would perceive them. And he was right.

'There was another man in the *Casa Reposada*,' said Goudini.

'Yes, I saw him.'

'You *knew* him?'

'I thought I did. I thought he was a man I knew in France many years ago, but when I accosted him he denied it.'

Goudini's eyes narrowed. His tone became menacing. 'He gave you something—a paper to take to England.'

'Señor Goudini,' replied Biggles wearily, 'I have already told you that we are here through force of circumstances, not through choice. If you think we have something, a paper or whatever it is, I suggest that you endeavour to find it. We are at your disposal, but please do not delay us too long because our clothes, as you may see for yourself, are wet, and we are anxious to dry them. We are also anxious to get to the Consulate, in order to obtain the necessary papers to take us across the frontier into France, from where we can get a train home.'

The hunchback rose abruptly to his feet and gave a swift order in Spanish. The other men advanced upon the prisoners and began stripping their clothes from them. When they were completely denuded they were taken into the bathroom, one of the men remaining with them. To this they submitted without protest, more than a little thankful that they had disposed of the document.

Twenty minutes passed, during which time their clothes were thoroughly searched, as was the room itself, and the bathroom. Goudini then announced in a voice charged with anger that they could put their clothes on again. This they did, finding the task by no means pleasant, for their garments were now cold as well as damp. When this was done the hunchback walked towards the door, beckoning them to follow.

'May I ask where you are taking us?' inquired Biggles.

'Yes, I am taking you to the prison,' replied the hunchback, coughing and spitting into the fireplace. 'In the prison you will either recover your memory, or—you will not,' he said suavely.

'But you can't do that,' protested Biggles. 'We are British subjects. I demand to see the British Vice-Consul.'

'You may be British subjects but you are now in Republican Spain,' returned Goudini icily. 'In any case, there would be no purpose served in taking you to the British consulate.'

'Why not?'

'Because it was struck by a bomb two days ago and completely wrecked,' returned the hunchback evenly. 'All those within were killed,' he added.

Biggles caught his breath. 'That is very unfortunate,' he said bitterly.

'Very unfortunate indeed—for you,' agreed Goudini. 'Not that it would make any difference. Come.'

The whole party went down the stairs and out through the front entrance to where the car was waiting. The body of the murdered man, and his car, had disappeared. The three airmen were told to get in. A word to the driver and Goudini and his assistants followed. The car sped away through the now quiet streets. A quarter of an hour's drive and it pulled up outside a forbidding-looking building. There was no need to ask what it was. Half a dozen members of the famous Catalonian *Guardia Civil** stood at the massive double doors; they moved aside to allow the car to enter.

The car stopped again at a smaller door within, and the occupants got out. There was a brief wait, and then a small, pompous-looking officer of senior rank arrived. Goudini spoke to him in low tones for a few moments and then returned to where the prisoners were standing. 'Perhaps you remember the paper now?' he suggested quietly.

'You will be sorry for this,' retorted Biggles grimly.

Goudini bowed slightly. '*Adios, caballeros***,*' he said, and re-entered the waiting car. An escort of guards, in their curious flat black hats, closed on the prisoners. A short march along a stone corridor and they were pushed into a fairly roomy cell. The door slammed and a heavy bolt shot home.

Biggles sat down on one of the several trestle beds which comprised the only furniture in the cell. 'We've had what you might call a fairly active day, haven't we?' he observed cheerfully.

---

* Civil police guards—one of the most celebrated police forces in the world. Like most continental police, they are armed like soldiers.
** Spanish: goodbye, gentlemen

Chapter 7
A Nasty Shock

Algy joined him on the bed. 'Yes,' he agreed, 'we have done quite a lot of hard work. I don't mind that, but what annoys me is that we don't seem to be making much progress. We've been in a few jams in our time, but this is about the stickiest. I'm not usually given to pessimism, but I'm dashed if I can see any way out of it—can you?'

'Don't be impatient,' smiled Biggles. 'I haven't looked yet.'

'Can you think of any way of getting out of this dungeon, for a start, because if so I'd like to hear it,' continued Algy. 'I'm hungry, I'm tired, and I'm slightly damp.'

'So am I. So are we all.'

'And as far as I can see we're likely to remain so,' murmured Algy. 'If you can get us out of this hole, I shall tell the world that you are a very clever fellow.'

'In that case I shall have to see what can be done about it,' grinned Biggles.

'Go right ahead,' Algy told him.

'Oh, shut up, Algy,' put in Ginger. 'What's come over you? We've got out of worse messes than this. Let's get down to brass tacks. The only way we shall get out of here is by breaking out or giving old stick-in-the-mud the letter.'

'Don't flatter yourself that giving Goudini the letter will get us out,' Biggles told him.

'But he said—'

'Yes, I know what he said. Forget it. Once he gets his hands on the letter he'll have all the more reason for keeping us here.'

'How do you make that out?'

'Do you suppose he is going to let us go back to London and report what happened to Frazer? Is he going to let us tell the Foreign Office that he, Goudini, has got the letter? Not likely. And don't overlook the point that we might have memorized the contents of the letter for all he knows. It's my opinion that our only chance lies in Goudini *not* finding the letter. Once he's got it, the sooner we are where we can't tell tales the better it would suit him.'

'That's cheerful.'

'It's no use blinking at facts.'

'You don't think he believed your story? It sounded pretty good to me.'

'It probably sounded pretty good to Goudini, but there were one or two things unexplained, and he didn't overlook them.'

'Such as?'

'The envelope. He found the envelope in that fellow's pocket after he was shot. Where could he have got the envelope from but from us? I think it's pretty certain that Goudini knows that we know more about the letter than we pretend.'

'What's it all about, anyway?' murmured Algy.

'I think it's pretty clear,' returned Biggles thoughtfully. 'Frazer is—or was, until he was killed—a secret agent. He picked up an important document—in Rome, I imagine, judging from what the fellow with the car said. He was followed to Barcelona. The Spanish Secret Service, headed by Goudini, got wind of it.

Frazer, possibly because he knew that it was going to be difficult for him to get out of Spain, arranged with another agent to take the letter home. The rendezvous was the *Casa Reposada*. We know what happened there. The messenger was murdered. Frazer, realizing that Goudini and Co. were outside waiting for him, took a desperate chance that we might get through.'

'Why didn't Goudini walk straight into the *Casa Reposada* and arrest him, I wonder?' murmured Ginger.

Biggles shook his head. 'That's something we don't know. Perhaps his own plans weren't ready. No doubt he would have come in if Frazer hadn't gone out. He could watch him through the window, so there was no fear of his getting away.'

'I wonder what happened to poor Frazer.'

'I'm afraid there isn't much doubt about that. They shot him as he went out. It looks as if they must have spotted us speaking to him. Although we were blissfully unaware of it, it seems that several people were taking a great interest in the pub which we unfortunately chose for a drink. Our trouble was that we never got a fair start. We were up against it from the very beginning. I doubt very much if we should ever have got away from the *Casa Reposada* if that fellow hadn't come along with his car. From what he said he was just a mercenary, playing his own game, which might be true, or it might not. You can never be sure of anything in this spy racket. He's finished with it now, anyway.'

'And here we are,' murmured Ginger.

'Precisely,' agreed Biggles.

'What's Goudini up to now, do you think?'

'I should say he is pulling that room in the hotel to pieces, looking for the letter. He knows that it went in there. He knows that the man who took us there hadn't got it on him when he came out. He knows that we haven't got it on us. It must therefore seem to him that it is still there. When he discovers that it isn't, not being a fool he will realize that we managed to dispose of it. When he reaches that point he will come back here, I fancy, and apply more drastic measures to induce us to produce it.'

'So what?' asked Ginger.

'That is something we shall know more about presently,' answered Biggles.

'Is it any use asking them to dry our clothes, do you suppose?'

'I shouldn't think so. Mine are getting dry on me, anyway. We might tell the jailer that we could do with a spot of food, though.' As he finished speaking Biggles walked over to the heavy door and hammered on it with his fists.

After a short delay it was opened and two members of the *Guardia Civil* appeared.

'*Comida*,' demanded Biggles pointing to his mouth. 'Food—*pan*—hungry.'

The men smiled faintly and departed, locking the door behind them.

'Not knowing the language properly doesn't make things any easier,' complained Biggles. 'They seemed to understand what I meant though. What's outside here, I wonder?' he continued, walking over to the window, where the others joined him.

It was small and heavily barred, and it did not take them long to ascertain that escape that way was out of the question, for the bars were thick and firmly embedded in the stonework. There was just sufficient light to enable them to see that they overlooked a wide, gravelled courtyard, not unlike a barrack square. In spite of

60

the hour, a few uniformed figures were walking across it in various directions, evidently engaged on some duty.

Biggles glanced at the sky. 'It will pretty soon be getting light,' he remarked.

'This place is going to take a bit of getting out of, I'm afraid,' muttered Ginger, who was now examining the bare walls.

'The main idea about a prison is to make it difficult for people to get out,' replied Biggles. 'The usual thing in books is for the place to be littered with trap doors, secret tunnels, and whatnots. Either that, or the bars in the window are conveniently loose. But this happens to be a modern prison, and as is usually the case with modern prisons, unofficial exits have been omitted.'

'Sure! You bet I will,' came a cheerful voice from the direction of the window.

Biggles sprang round as if he had been stung. 'Who said that?' he asked.

'It's somebody talking outside,' flashed back Ginger.

They all ran to the window.

A few paces away two soldiers were engaged in conversation.

'They're English,' whispered Algy tersely.

'Americans—or one of them is,' corrected Biggles. 'They must be légionnaires*. There are all sorts of nationals here, fighting for the Spanish government. Hey, Buddy!' he called.

The man who was speaking broke off short; he looked quickly at the window.

'Come over here; I want to speak to you,' went on Biggles.

* Foreign volunteers fighting for the Spanish Government loyalists against Franco.

One of the men, after a few words to his companion, turned and walked away. The other came to the window and smiled through the bars. 'Say, what's the idea?' he asked. 'Are you from the States?'

'No,' Biggles told him quickly. 'We're British, and we're in a mess. We came ashore off a boat and got picked up by the cops. They took us for spies and popped us in here.'

'Too bad. Why don't you send word to your consul?'

'No use. The consulate was blown up a couple of days ago.'

'Say, that's not so good.'

'You're right, it isn't. How about doing a pal a good turn?'

'What do you want me to do—get shot for trying to get you out?'

'Of course not; but if we had a file or a hacksaw we could get out ourselves.'

'Are you guys on the level?'

'As level as a billiard table,' declared Biggles. 'It's all a mistake, but we can't make the cops see that. Not being able to talk the lingo makes it harder. Come on, be a pal, or as like as not they'll leave us here till the end of the war.'

The légionnaire took a furtive glance around. 'I don't carry files about with me,' he said.

'But I reckon you could get hold of one if you wanted to.'

'Maybe.' The légionnaire hesitated, while the prisoners, realizing how much hung on his decision, held their breath. 'Okay,' he said at last. 'I'll see what I can do; but don't you pull me into this.'

'Whatever happens you'll be left out,' swore Biggles.

'See you later, maybe,' said the légionnaire, and after a glance round, walked quickly away.

'By gosh, that was a bit of luck!' muttered Ginger in an excited whisper. 'I—' He broke off as a key rattled in the door, and one of the guards entered with a tray.

'Thanks,' cried Biggles cheerfully, eyeing a loaf of bread, some cheese, and a jug of coffee. '*Gracias, señor, gracias**.'

The guard who was carrying the tray put it down on a bed, and then withdrew.

No cutlery had been provided, so Biggles seized the long Spanish loaf and broke it into three parts. 'This is better,' he declared. 'Things are looking up.'

'If that American—' began Ginger, but Biggles interrupted him.

'Not so fast with the American,' he said quietly.

'What do you mean?'

'That fellow may have spoken English like an American, but I'll bet my boots that he isn't one,' declared Biggles firmly. 'Didn't you notice the little lisp behind the vowels? I should say that he is either a Spaniard who has lived in the States, or a South American from Argentina.'

'It doesn't matter, does it, as long as he brings us a file?'

'Not a bit—but I wouldn't reckon too much on the file. There was something about that fellow that I didn't like. I merely mention it so that you won't be surprised if the file doesn't arrive. If it does, then I'll apologize mentally for doubting him,' concluded Biggles.

He had only just finished speaking when there came

---

* Spanish: Thank you, Sir, thank you.

63

a quiet rap on one of the window bars. 'Say, are you guys still there?' came the voice of the man they had just been discussing.

'We certainly are,' replied Biggles, hurrying to the window.

'Okay, boys—there she is,' came the voice from outside the window.

Biggles picked up a small but efficient-looking hacksaw. When he looked back at the window the man had gone.

'Gosh! He didn't waste any time,' remarked Ginger.

'I'll take back all I said about him,' answered Biggles. 'We all make mistakes sometimes. You two go on eating while I start on the middle bar. When you have finished, come and take over while I have a bite. We've no time to lose; I reckon it will be light in an hour.' With that he set to work on the centre bar, muffling his jacket round it to deaden the sound.

He was nearly through it when Algy relieved him, so he went over to what remained of the food and ate it ravenously, taking the precaution, however, of placing Ginger on guard with his ear to the door in case any one came to remove the tray. The men who had brought the food did, in fact, return shortly afterwards, but Ginger having given warning of their approach, the prisoners had ample time to throw themselves on their beds in attitudes of passive resignation. But the footsteps of the guards had no sooner died away than they were hard at it again, taking it in turn to use the hacksaw so that they could expend the maximum amount of energy.

The tool bit into the soft iron so readily that in three-quarters of an hour two bars—which they thought would provide an opening large enough for them to get through—were held in place only by the merest thread of metal. A few seconds would be enough to remove them altogether.

Biggles glanced at the sky and noted that it was turning grey. 'We are only just in time,' he said. 'I reckon this square will be stiff with people as soon as it gets light, so we had better be moving while there is nobody about.'

The two bars were swiftly cut through and placed quietly on the floor. Another minute and the prisoners were outside, standing close against the wall taking stock of their surroundings.

'That looks like the main entrance over there,' observed Biggles in an undertone. 'I don't suppose there's another exit, so we shall have to try our luck.' He started walking quickly down the side of the square on which they had emerged.

'That's the gate, right enough,' murmured Ginger a moment later. 'But it looks to me as if it's shut.'

'I was afraid of that,' rejoined Biggles. 'But if it's the only way out we've got to try to get through it. One thing is certain: the longer we remain inside, the less chance we shall have of getting out. If those guards come back for any reason and find that we have gone, this place will be buzzing like a beehive inside five minutes.'

As he spoke Biggles glanced across at the far side of the square and saw that several soldiers were emerging in a desultory fashion from a small door. 'It looks as if this place is a barracks as well as a prison,' he said tersely. 'I should say those troops are turning out for early morning parade. Judging by their uniforms they are légionnaires. If—' He broke off suddenly as two officers appeared round an angle of the wall a short distance in front of them. There was no question of avoiding them, for the officers had already seen them and were regarding them curiously.

Biggles took the bull by the horns. He walked straight on until he was face to face with the officers. 'Pardon,' he said, 'but does either of you gentlemen speak English?'

'*Français*,' answered one of them curtly.

'Good!' returned Biggles. 'Then would you please have the goodness to direct me?' he went on quickly, speaking in French. 'We have come to join the legion. Can you show us the headquarters or the stores where we may draw our uniforms?'

'There is the quartermaster's stores over there,' answered the officer to whom Biggles had addressed the question. He pointed to a section of the building near to where the troops were rapidly assembling. Then with a nod he strode off in that direction.

'*Merci, mon Capitaine**,*' said Biggles, and started walking briskly in the direction indicated. 'There seem to be as many foreigners in Barcelona as there are Spaniards,' he observed, throwing a glance over his shoulder to see if they were being watched. 'It shouldn't be difficult to get hold of some uniforms; if we can do that the rest should be easy. This is the place, I think. Leave me to do the talking.'

They found a Spanish N.C.O.** in charge of the stores, and Biggles' nostrils twitched as they were assailed by the reek of garlic. 'We are new recruits for the legion,' he began. 'Do you speak English?'

'I speak English like the Spanish,' returned the N.C.O. proudly. 'Also the Italian and the French. That

* French: Thank you, Captain.
** Non-Commissioned Officer, e.g. a Corporal or a Sergeant.

is why I am here, a sergeant of the International Brigade*. Jolly good! Pedro—that's me. Yes, I am here.'

'I had noticed that,' replied Biggles seriously, repressing a smile. 'Every one said, "Find Pedro—he'll fix you up." '

'Yes, I fix everybody up,' declared the Spaniard warmly. 'With you I make my best fixings.'

'That's fine,' Biggles told him. 'What about some uniforms?'

The store-keeper eyed him reflectively. 'I go now for my coffee—not half,' he answered vaguely. 'You come back sometime and we make the fixings; so long good-bye.'

Biggles remained calm. He took a hundred-peseta note from his pocket and smoothed it out. 'We have come a long way and we cannot waste time,' he said. 'The captain is waiting.'

The Spaniard shrugged his shoulders. 'Quite right,' he said, taking the note from Biggles' fingers with an apologetic air. 'Help yourself,' he went on, indicating the stores with a wave of his hand. 'I go for coffee, you bet. When I come back you have the fixings. If any one comes you say that Pedro has gone for coffee. All right. *Adios*'.

'*Adios*,' echoed Biggles. Then, as the Spaniard went out of the door, he added quickly in a low voice, 'Make it snappy. We've got to get out of this place pretty soon or we never shall get out.'

No further time was wasted in discussion. There were plenty of uniforms from which to choose, many

* The International Brigade consisted of volunteers from many nations, organized by the World Communist movement to fight for the government loyalist forces.

67

in a filthy condition, obviously having already seen service. But Biggles was not particular. He soon found one to fit him, and the others did the same. 'We might as well do the thing properly,' he advised, kicking off his flimsy shoes and replacing them with boots. An ammunition belt completed the outfit, and he turned to the door. 'All clear,' he said. 'Let's go.'

In line abreast they marched boldly towards the main gate, around which some soldiers, presumably the guard, were lounging, their rifles propped against the wall. They took not the slightest notice of the three pseudo-légionnaires* as they marched past them through the gate and out on to the road—not that there was any reason why they should, for troops were coming in and out all the time.

'By gosh, we've done it!' whispered Ginger.

'Keep going,' Biggles told him under his breath.

Not until they had turned the corner did he slacken his pace.

'What now?' asked Algy.

'We've got to get the paper.'

'It's likely to take us some time to find the place.'

'I know the name of the hotel. I noted it as we went in. It is the Hotel Valencia. A taxi will be the easiest way to get there, if we can find one.'

Biggles looked up and down the street, but without seeing what he sought.

They walked some distance without success, from which Biggles concluded that the taxis had been commandeered for military service. They were just abandoning hope of finding any sort of vehicle when an ancient cab, drawn by an emaciated horse, came round

* Phoney legionnaires

the corner. Biggles held up his hand and the driver stopped. 'Hotel Valencia,' he said, and the driver indicated by a wave of his hand that he knew where it was.

The drive that followed seemed interminable, for in spite of the driver's whip-cracking and exhortations, the wretched animal could only amble at the best. It stumbled often, and on one occasion nearly fell. Ginger, incensed by this apparent cruelty to animals, began to expostulate, but Biggles silenced him. 'Keep quiet,' he said. 'You'll see plenty of this in Spain. You'll do no good by kicking up a row, so just forget about it.'

At length the long journey came to an end, and Biggles stopped the cab as soon as he realized that they were in the avenue in which the hotel was situated. 'We shall be less likely to attract attention if we walk,' he said quietly, after he had paid the driver. 'There seems to be nobody about, so finding the paper ought to be easy.'

Biggles' optimism seemed justified, for not a soul was in sight as they walked briskly past the hotel entrance to the waste plot of land beyond. Biggles stopped when they reached it. 'There's no need for us all to go,' he said. 'Ginger, you stay here and keep cave. Whistle if you see any one coming.' With that he hurried forward.

'I can see it,' he told Algy a moment later. 'Thank goodness! I had a horrible feeling it might not be there.' Stooping, he picked up the well-remembered ball of newspaper, and tearing it open, removed the ornament from the inside. He was about to take out the paper when a warning shout made him start round. Something between a snarl and an ejaculation broke from his lips.

From all sides men in the uniform of the *Guardia Civil* were closing in on them.

Biggles' face turned pale. 'Ten thousand devils seize that hunchback!' he snapped. 'He laid a trap for us and we've walked straight into it.'

A score of rifles menaced them as the armed police advanced at a run. An order rang out.

Suddenly Biggles swung round. 'Ginger!' he roared. 'Catch!' and he hurled the ornament high into the air over the heads of the police.

Ginger, judging his distance, darted forward. For a moment he stood rigid, crouching like a cricketer waiting for a ball.

Biggles held his breath.

So did Ginger, as his eyes watched the curving flight of the ornament. Time seemed to stand still. Then, somehow, the image was in his hands, and he was streaking down the avenue like a rabbit making for its burrow with a terrier at its heels. Subconsciously he heard shouts, shots, and the scream of ricocheting bullets. He also heard Biggles' wild yell of 'Well caught!' A narrow passage appeared on his left, and he sped down it like a pickpocket with the police on his heels.

Chapter 8
Ginger Goes Alone

Ginger ran on in a daze, bewildered by the suddenness of the calamity that had separated him from the others. So, hardly knowing what he was doing, he ran blindly, nearly distraught with anxiety for the others and horrified by the responsibility that now rested on him. He was still clutching the ornament in his right hand when it occurred to him that it would be safer in his pocket. In trying to accomplish this it slipped from his fingers and crashed to pieces on the hard road. Snatching up the precious letter, he thrust it into his pocket, and then, seeing no signs of hue and cry, slowed down to a walk. Somewhere not far away a bugle was blowing a series of short, jerky calls, but he paid no attention to it.

He was just congratulating himself on having got clear away when the sound of running footsteps made him throw a nervous glance over his shoulder. He saw at once that his worst fears were realized. Two soldiers were coming after him at a run. They let out a shout when they saw him turn. That was quite enough for Ginger, who resumed his flight incontinently.

Panting, he burst round the next corner, only to pull up with a cry of dismay, for not fifty yards ahead were fully a dozen soldiers. The fact that they were hurrying in the same direction as he was made no difference to Ginger—the sight of any sort of uniform was enough to induce alarm; and while he stood staring about him wildly, seeking in vain for an avenue of escape, the two soldiers appeared round the corner behind him so that he was now between two fires, so to speak.

In his emotion Ginger went as far as to contemplate the destruction of the letter, if only to prevent it from falling into Goudini's hands. In fact, he had already put his hand into his pocket with that object in view when the soldiers in front broke into a run and disappeared round a corner, so he ran after them rather than be overtaken by those behind, who were obviously pursuing him—or so he thought. But when he reached the corner, and saw what lay ahead, he recoiled with a gasp of despair. It was a wide square, and it was swarming with soldiers, all surging towards a line of motor transport that stood under some trees on the far side.

It had just occurred to Ginger that no one was taking any notice of him when a heavy hand fall upon his shoulder from behind. Jerking round, he came face to face with a soldier who said something in a language he did not understand, although, naturally, he assumed that it was Spanish.

'What—what—?' he gasped.

A second soldier, a little fellow with a brown, alert face, who had been hurrying on, swung round. 'Blimey!' said a cockney voice. ''Ullo, mate, are you one of our mob?'

Ginger stared. He began to think that he was going out of his mind. Slowly it dawned upon him that his fears had been groundless; that the soldiers had no designs against him. 'Are you English?' he asked, and then realized how foolish the question sounded.

'No; I'm the King of China,' grinned the cockney, his bright eyes twinkling, and then roared with laughter at his joke. 'Fred Summers, from Plaistow—that's me. How's yerself?'

Ginger smiled wanly. He felt weak with relief. 'I'm Ginger Hebblethwaite from Yorkshire,' he said. 'What's going on here?'

'Going on! Blimey, that's good. Didn't yer hear the alarm? They say the spaghetti-wallahs are busting our line, so back we go.'

'You mean—Italians—General Franco's Italians?'

'What else do yer fink I mean? Come on.'

'I see,' replied Ginger vaguely, beginning to suspect that he had jumped out of the frying-pan into the fire. 'I'm new here,' he explained.

'Well, that's all right, mate; you stick to me,' said the generous-hearted cockney confidently. 'I'll show yer round.'

'Round—round where?' Ginger asked the question, although in his heart he knew the answer.

'The trenches, of course. Come on.'

'But—but just a minute,' stammered Ginger. 'You don't understand. I—no, I'm going this way.' He started to back away, for he had no intention of going to a war about which he knew little, and cared less, if he could avoid it. But a brawny sergeant with a waxed moustache cut him off, and bundled the two of them towards the waiting transport.

'That's Froggy,' whispered Summers. 'He's a hot 'un, he is. They say he was in the French Foreign Legion in Africa before he came here, and I shouldn't wonder at it the way he goes on. You watch your step with 'im.'

But Ginger was barely listening. In a kind of dream he took the rifle that was thrust into his hands, and put some packets of cartridges into the pouch on his

73

belt. But he was still thinking of escape. Twice he tried to break away, but each time the French sergeant, who seemed to suspect his intention, called him back, and he dared not risk it again. For the present, at any rate, he would have to obey orders, that was clear; so he climbed into one of the lorries with his new-found friend. A jabber of foreign languages fell on his ears; the reek of garlic hung in the dust-laden air.

'You'll be all right, mate, don't worry,' said Summers cheerfully, noticing Ginger's downcast expression. 'I'll keep an eye on you.'

'Thanks,' replied Ginger wearily, and sank down on a pile of equipment to try to think calmly, for the rush of events had carried him off his feet. Only one thing seemed to matter at the moment, and that was that he was on his way to the front with the letter in his pocket, not knowing whether Biggles and Algy were alive or dead. Even if they were alive they might never know what had become of him, he reflected miserably. And the more he thought about it, the more hopeless did the situation appear.

His morbid thoughts, pardonable in the circumstances, were interrupted by the forward movement of the lorry. A great crowd of women and girls were cheering themselves hoarse; the troops replied by blowing kisses and singing snatches of songs; but Ginger only stared glumly into the sea of faces. 'Anybody would think we were going to a beanfeast,' he thought bitterly.

Once clear of the square the lorry increased its speed, and soon they were racing down a dusty road between groves of olive trees and far-spreading vineyards beyond. Women ran out of the houses they passed and cheered the troops on their way. Ginger, still determined to return at the first opportunity, settled down

74

to watch for landmarks. There was nothing else he could do.

He realized that he hardly knew what the war in Spain was about. It had never interested him. He had a vague idea that it was a civil war in which certain other countries had taken sides, but since he did not even know the original cause of the quarrel he had no sympathies with either side. In fact, it made the whole idea of taking part in the war more repugnant. He was deadly tired. So much had happened since the ship had been bombed; it seemed weeks since he slept in a bed. Twice he caught himself dozing; and each time he pulled himself together with a start, for he was still trying to follow the direction the lorry was taking. He settled down a little lower on the equipment. Some one put a folded blanket under his head, and looking up, he saw that it was the friendly little cockney. He smiled his thanks. The landscape became a blurred picture of gnarled grey olives, black, pencil-like cypresses, and rolling fields of grapes, under a sky of heavenly blue. He was very warm and comfortable. His eyes closed and this time they did not open.

When he awoke he noticed that the lorry had stopped, and he realized that it was the jerk that had awakened him. For a moment he could not remember what had happened; then memory surged into his brain and he stared about him in alarm. The clear, pale, eggshell blue tint of the sky told him that the afternoon had far advanced, and he was still marvelling that he could have slept so long when the muzzle of a rifle prodded his ribs, and he scrambled round to see 'Froggy' gesticulating at him. With a guilty start he saw that most of the troops had already dismounted, and were lining up a short distance away, so picking up his rifle he jumped down and joined them.

Fred Summers saw him coming and hurried to meet him. 'I was just coming back for you,' he said. 'They got me out first to unload some stuff. Well, 'ere we are. What do yer fink of it? Bit different from old 'Ampstead 'Eath, ain't it?'

'Yes, it certainly is,' agreed Ginger, staring about him wonderingly, for while he had been asleep the landscape had changed. No longer the smiling fields of grapes. All around, gaunt mountains thrust their peaks high into the clear sky. He was still staring when a machine-gun started its hateful chatter not far away.

'What's that?' he asked.

'What, ain't yer never 'eard a machine-gun before?' was the surprised answer.

'Yes, of course,' answered Ginger. 'I didn't exactly mean that. I meant—what is it shooting at?'

'Franco, I 'ope.'

'But—'

'The trenches are just round that next hill,' explained Summers. 'Things are pretty quiet just at this minute, or you'd 'ave known all about it. I've bin 'ere before, and it's a hot shop. There's a big river called the Ebro just round the corner; that's where all the fuss is going on. They say Franco is trying to get across.'

'I see,' said Ginger vaguely. He was still by no means clear as to what was happening beyond the fact that he had arrived at the front and that a battle in which he would be expected to take part was imminent. The knowledge depressed him; he realized that to try to get away now would probably see him brought before a firing-squad and condemned to death for cowardice; but he was resolved nevertheless to seize the first oppor-

76

tunity of getting back to Barcelona. Had Biggles and Algy been there he would not have minded so much; in fact, he might have found the experience interesting; but with their fate weighing heavily upon him he could take no interest in anything. 'I'll get back somehow,' he told himself desperately.

Further rumination was interrupted by a general stir in the ranks as N.C.O.s hurried up and down getting the troops into column. An order was barked, and the regiment broke into a marching-song as it tramped up the dusty road towards its allotted station. Ginger did not sing. He did not even know the language in which the song was being sung. In any case, the last thing he felt like doing was singing; on the contrary, he fumed inwardly at the unfortunate series of accidents that had resulted in the present alarming situation. Nevertheless, once he smiled a grim smile, in which there was little humour, as he recalled that Biggles had started off originally on what was intended to be a spot of rest cure.

He turned envious eyes upwards as an aeroplane, a mere speck in the sky, droned across their line on an unknown errand.

'Curse that organ-grinder,' muttered Summers at Ginger's elbow, nodding towards the 'plane.

'It's one of Franco's machines, then?' asked Ginger, for he did not recognize the type.

'One o' them Fiats.' (He pronounced it Fyats, but Ginger knew what he meant.) 'I've seen plenty of 'em. So'll you. If he's spotted us we shall know all about it soon enough.'

Presently a shell whined overhead and burst about two hundred yards beyond the marching column.

77

'There y'are. What did I tell yer?' snarled Summers. 'You watch the rookies turn green.'

Ginger noticed that several of the men around him had turned pale, and realized that they were under fire for the first time. He himself felt a sinking feeling in the pit of the stomach.

Another shell wailed towards them, and Ginger was not the only one who ducked as it burst viciously in the air just short of the troops.

'Shrapnel*,' growled Summers laconically. 'Here comes another.'

The shell burst some distance ahead, and Ginger grasped the fact that the 'plane now circling high overhead was correcting the gunners' aim.

'We shall get it in the neck as soon as they get our range,' murmured Summers casually.

'That's right. Be cheerful,' returned Ginger, who was feeling distinctly uncomfortable.

Before Summers could resume the conversation an order had sent the column forward at a brisk double, which was maintained until they entered a narrow defile** in the mountains. Ginger caught his breath as they entered it and his eyes fell on a line of wounded men lying beside the path. A doctor and an orderly were busily at work. One of the unfortunate fellows was groaning horribly, and Ginger looked away.

'You'll see plenty o' that,' remarked Summers calmly. 'Yer soon get used to it, though.'

Ginger was not comforted. He kept his eyes to the front, and breathed a sigh of relief as the head of the

* Artillery shell containing bullets or pieces of metal called shrapnel set to burst above the ground.
** A narrow passage through which troops can only march one behind the other.

78

column turned into a deep trench cut in the side of the defile. He caught a glimpse of open country and a wide river some distance below and ahead of them.

'This is the communication trench,' announced Summers. 'Looks like we're going straight into the front line.'

This expectation proved to be correct, for after proceeding for some distance, during which time the sound of rifle fire grew rapidly nearer, the troops, now in single file, entered a narrow trench that ran at right angles to the communication trench. Men, gaunt and unshaven, were leaning against the far side, firing between sandbags and lumps of rock. Some paid no attention to the newcomers; others grinned and threw coarse jokes over their shoulders.

''Ere we are,' remarked Summers. He might have been announcing their arrival at a London terminus, so dispassionate was his tone of voice.

Ginger wondered what curious urge had induced the little cockney to abandon peace and security for a war, the result of which could make no possible difference to him. The same could be said of nearly all the other members of the International Brigade.

They had come to a halt, because the men in front of them had stopped, and Ginger realized from the way they dropped their equipment, loosened their collars and made themselves at home, as it were, that this was his destination. He leaned his rifle against the side of the trench, and walked towards a wide opening in order to see what lay beyond—a step that was, in the circumstances, quite natural. He did actually reach the opening, and was staring down a steep bank below when Summers caught his arm and dragged him aside just as something thudded into the rear wall of the trench.

'What yer trying to do—commit suicide?' asked Summers, in a voice that was heavy with sarcasm.

Ginger gazed at him wide-eyed. 'My goodness! I didn't realize—' he began, but Summers cut him short.

'You won't realize anything long if you go shovin' yer 'ead through 'oles in the parapet,' he said severely. 'Take my tip and keep yer skull down till you're told to do something.'

Ginger stepped aside to permit the passage of two medical orderlies carrying a stretcher between them. On it lay the body of a middle-aged man. He had been shot through the head.

Ginger turned a white face to his new-found comrade. 'This is awful,' he said in a hollow voice.

'What—this?' Summers smiled. 'Why, this ain't nothin'. You wait. Come on, mate. Let's go and find our bivvy* and get fixed up.'

Ginger followed the cockney down the trench.

---

* Slang: bivouac, a temporary open-air encampment without tents.

Chapter 9
A Lucky Combat

For two days Ginger suffered all the agonies of fear and horror inseparable from modern trench warfare, to which was added a gnawing anxiety every time he thought of Biggles and Algy, or the document that still reposed in his pocket; with the passing of time the chances of its ever being delivered became more and more remote.

There were times, however, when he forgot everything except the desperate business of preserving his own life, for on two occasions the enemy—for so he had come to regard the troops in the trenches opposite to them—had made determined attacks that had only been repulsed after bitter fighting and heavy casualties on both sides. At such times he had fought as furiously as the comrades who lined the parapet on either side of him; he had no choice in the matter, for while the war, as far as he was concerned, was an impersonal matter, the success of the attacking troops would in all probability see the end of him; in which case the letter he carried would never reach its destination. So he found himself a position on the firestep, and fired at the attackers with a grim zeal that won the admiration of the cockney friend to whom he had already become attached. Each attack had been preceded by a bombardment from the enemy's artillery, and machine gunnery by General Franco's airmen, which the troops in the trenches could do little or nothing to prevent.

Ginger had fired at several enemy machines, and his inability to check their progress had aroused in him a wholehearted hatred of the enemy pilots who—so it seemed to him—dealt death with little risk to themselves.

Not that his own side was without aircraft. Spellbound, he had watched several dog-fights high in the air above, but he saw that the enemy machines were usually superior in performance to those of his own side, with the result that most of the combats ended in the enemy's favour. How he longed to be seated in one of the cockpits can be better imagined than described, for as far as he could see, in that way, and that way only, lay the mobility that meant freedom. Yet, situated as he was, an aeroplane seemed as unattainable as the moon.

He had learned to recognize one of their own machines, a squat, blunt-nosed fighter, painted blue. He had seen it several times high up; on one such occasion he had joined in a yell of triumph that arose from his trench when it had sent an Italian Fiat toppling out of the sky, to crash in flames near the river below. But that morning, shortly after dawn, during the height of the enemy's attack, it had appeared low down, and racing along the lines, had sprayed the attacking troops with its machine-guns to such good effect that it had unquestionably been a deciding factor of the battle. Ginger's interest had been all the more amplified when Fred Summers had told him that the 'Blue Devil'—for by this name the machine was known to the troops—was flown by one Jock McLannock, a wild Scotsman from Glasgow, a pilot of high social position who had abandoned his Highland home to fight in what he considered to be the cause of freedom and justice—a cause for which millions of men since the beginning of time have laid down their lives, usually in vain.

The attack had failed, and the Blue Devil had withdrawn to its distant aerodrome; the trench had settled down to its usual routine, leaving Ginger to contemplate his position with melancholy forebodings. These were not without justification. He had seen many men killed; already he had had more than one narrow escape, and it seemed to him that it was only a question of time before a bullet found a billet in his body. It was not so much that he was afraid of dying; what really upset him was the thought of being killed without Biggles and Algy ever hearing of his fate; that, and the fact that the letter, obviously of vital importance, could never then be delivered to those who probably even then were anxiously awaiting its arrival.

He did not, of course, abandon hope. On the contrary, he had racked his brains for some way of getting out of the trenches as a first move in the difficult task of making contact with Biggles and Algy, or ascertaining what had become of them. Vigilant eyes were ever on the watch for deserters, who, so he was told, were shot out of hand, and the expedient of trying to make an escape was fraught with such deadly danger that he dared not risk it. Sooner or later—so Summers had told him—the regiment would be given a rest, either in a camp behind the lines, or in Barcelona, where it had been, in fact, when enemy activity had caused it to be recalled, and Ginger had been caught in the rally.

He thought of asking to be transferred to the Air Force, and would have done so had he been able to explain his position and qualifications to the French sergeant or the Spanish commanding officer; but cautious inquiry had elicited the fact that neither of them spoke English, and as he could speak neither French nor Spanish, the difficulty seemed insurmountable. The last thing he wanted was to create an impression that he was looking for an excuse to get out of the line, for that would be more likely to make him an object of suspicion. Moreover, it might lead to embarrassing questions as to how he got where he was, which might easily result in investigations that would come to Goudini's notice. So he did nothing, deeming it expedient to wait for a chance that must—so he told himself with more hope than confidence—sooner or later turn up.

It was late in the afternoon when, sitting on a box of ammunition in the bottom of the trench cleaning his rifle, he was aroused from his task by the roar of aircraft overhead. Looking up, he saw an enemy two-seater approaching the lines from beyond the river, flying on a meandering course which suggested that it was engaged either on photography or reconnaissance. But, although the pilot was obviously unaware of it, he was not alone in the air. Roaring down in an almost vertical dive from a sky now soft with sunset hues came a single-seater; and it did not need Summers' shout to tell Ginger that it was the Blue Devil.

Thrilling with excitement, Ginger sprang to his feet to watch the combat that was imminent, for if such affairs aroused the enthusiasm of his comrades—and they certainly did—how much greater was the effect on him, an airman!

The pilot of the two-seater, and his gunner, were both guilty of gross carelessness. To Ginger's professional eyes there was no doubt whatever about that. Or it may have been that they were over-confident. Be that as it may, they were both caught napping, and the nimble scout got in a long burst of fire, which struck the larger machine, and from which it never fully recovered. It lurched, swerving as it did so, but almost as quickly recovered and turned, nose down, for the safety of its own lines.

But the fighting pilot had no intention of allowing it to escape. His dive had carried him down below the two-seater; but now, with the tremendous speed gained by the dive to add to the power of his engine, he whirled round and, guns chattering, zoomed up like a rocket under the tail of his victim.

The nose of the two-seater jerked up convulsively, an almost certain sign that the pilot had been hit. But still the machine did not fall. The engine cut out, and it settled down in a steep glide, its nose still pointing towards home.

It was clear to Ginger that the gunner in the two-seater did not lack courage, for he could see him swinging his gun this way and that as he strove frantically to bring it to bear on the Blue Devil, who was now pouring in burst after burst of fire from different angles, at a speed that gave the two-seater gunner little opportunity of getting a sight on him.

The larger machine was now clearly in a bad way; its glide had steepened into a dive, and its course had become so erratic that it seemed only a question of seconds before it went into a spin from which it certainly would not recover. And the pilot of the Blue Devil might well have let it go at that. But prudence plays little part in air fighting, and the Scotsman was clearly determined to finish what he had so well started. He had climbed above his victim, and now he rushed in to deliver what was no doubt intended to be the *coup de grâce**.

But now it was his turn to be guilty of an indiscretion—either that, or he under-estimated the valour of the gunner in the two-seater. Instead of remaining in the larger machine's blind spot, he allowed his dive to carry him up until he was almost alongside his quarry, thus giving the gunner an opportunity he was not slow to seize. Staggering to his feet, he dragged his gun round, and poured a withering blast of fire at his blue persecutor. At such a range he could hardly miss.

The wild exultant yells of triumph that had followed the combat from the trench in which Ginger stood fell to a breathless hush.

'Blimey!' gasped Summers, 'he's got 'it. Not 'arf 'e aint.'

Ginger did not answer. With parted lips he was watching the Blue Devil, now the only machine in the sky, for immediately following the gunner's last brilliant effort the two-seater had gone into a spin from which it did not recover until it crashed just beyond the river. A curious silence hung on the air, for the Blue Devil's engine had stopped. With stationary propeller, the machine was gliding back from the enemy lines, over which the fight had carried it, towards its own. It was, in fact, heading for the section of trenches held by the International Brigade.

'Maybe he'll be all right, after all,' exclaimed Summers, nervously.

Ginger shook his head. 'He'll never do it,' he said confidently. 'He's due for a crack up, anyway, when he comes down on the rocks. Even if he isn't hit I'm

* French: death blow.

afraid he's going to be knocked about when he strikes the carpet.'

The further the crippled machine glided the more clear it became that Ginger's estimate had been correct. The Blue Devil could not reach the front line trench. The pilot did his best—as he was bound to do in the circumstances—holding the machine in a steady, shallow glide, regardless of the rattle of musketry that followed it from the enemy trenches.

'Yes! He'll do it!' yelled Summers, dancing in his excitement. 'Come on, mate, come on!'

'He'll be at least fifty yards short,' replied Ginger calmly.

'Then he'll be potted before he can get in here,' declared Summers.

Ginger knew what he meant. The place where the Blue Devil would crash in another instant was in full view of the enemy trenches, and the artillery beyond them, so the machine and its pilot would be subject to a fire from which only a miracle could help them to escape.

The Blue Devil struck the sun-drenched rocks with a crash like a falling tree. Under the impact the landing-gear was torn off, but not before it had sent the fuselage bounding high into the air. For a moment it hung in space, wallowing like a fish out of water, and then came down on a wing-tip with another crash that ripped the wing off at its roots. The rest settled down with a splintering of three-ply. Then there was silence.

Ginger, rushing to a loophole in the parapet, saw that the crash lay about forty yards only from the place where he stood. Risking a sniper's bullet, he watched to see if the pilot was able to disentangle himself, but there was no sign of movement.

'You'll get a bullet through yer nob if yer stand there much longer,' warned Summers.

Ginger twisted away from the loophole, his brain in a whirl. 'He's trapped in the wreckage,' he cried hoarsely. 'I know he was all right coming down because I saw him moving; his head was over the side looking to see where he was going.'

'What abart it? Yer can't do nothin'.'

'I tell you he's only trapped,' cried Ginger again.

As if in confirmation, a faint hail came from where the crashed machine lay.

A ripple of excited conversation buzzed along the trench, but nobody did anything.

Ginger felt a wave of anger and indignation sweep through him, and the sound of rifle fire from the enemy trenches moved him to a sort of madness. Wild-eyed, he looked about him for an instrument that might be of service. The only thing he could see was the bayonet on his rifle. In an instant he had snatched it off and was scrambling up the parapet.

''Ere, what's the idea?' jerked out Summers in a startled voice.

Ginger did not answer. He flung himself over the parapet of sandbags, and staggering to his feet, ran like a hare towards the crash. There was no thought in his mind that he was performing a brave action; in fact, he hardly knew what he was doing. The action had been spontaneous. An airman, and as such, a comrade, was exposed to peril. It seemed, therefore, only a natural thing that he should do his best to rescue him. That this might in the end turn to his own advantage was the last thought in his mind, nor did it remotely occur to him that the incident might be the answer to his prayers.

With bullets whistling past his ears, or screaming off the rocks around his feet, he reached his objective, and saw at once that his suspicions were correct. The pilot was not only conscious, but was making strenuous efforts to free himself. What prevented this was a flying wire dragged taut across his chest, holding him in his seat. He rolled his eyes questioningly when Ginger arrived on the scene.

'Losh, mon, take care! Ye'll get shot.'

The advice fell on heedless ears. Ginger hacked on the wire with frantic energy. Even if he had been prepared to take care, it was not easy to see how this was to be done. 'Keep your hands clear or the wires may cut them,' he admonished the struggling pilot.

'Scotland for ever!' shouted the pilot of the Blue Devil.

'Scotland yourself; I'm English,' shouted Ginger, and with that he struck the wire such a tremendous blow that not only did the bayonet sever it but it came within an inch of taking the pilot's hand off. To complicate matters, at that moment a bullet hit the blade, striking it out of his hand with such force that his wrist was numbed, and he pitched clean over the fuselage on to the rocks on the other side. Half dazed, he was picking himself up when a hand seized him by the collar and dragged him with scant regard for bruises into a near by shell-hole.

In the bottom of this haven of refuge rescuer and rescued stared at each other. 'You asked for what you got,' snorted Ginger. 'You must have been daft to give that fellow such an easy shot.'

The Scotsman blinked. 'Are ye telling me how to fly, ye little whipper-snapper?' he roared.

'I am. But don't shout so loud,' returned Ginger.

'Let's get into the trench.' He started crawling up the side of the shell-hole, but the Scotsman dragged him back.

'Wait, mon! It's you that's daft. Listen.'

Ginger paused. Bullets were ripping through the machine. A shell sailed over and burst not far away, sending such a shower of broken rock into the air that the two occupants of the hole ducked and covered their heads with their hands.

'We'd do better to stay where we are until the fireworks are over,' announced the Scotsman. 'Ye haven't a drink on ye, I expect?'

Ginger shook his head as he crawled back to the bottom of the shell-hole. 'You're right,' he agreed. 'We'll wait until it's dark. It won't be long.'

The Scotsman took a paper packet of cigarettes from his pocket, and lighting one, sent a cloud of smoke into the air as he made himself as comfortable as the place would permit. 'This matter of me making a fool o' mysel'. Ye're an expert, na doot?'

Ginger ignored the sarcasm in the other's voice. 'No,' he said. 'But I watched the fight, and while I know that it's easy to sit on the carpet and criticize what somebody is doing upstairs, it seemed to me that you made a bloomer.'

'Ye're richt, laddie,' admitted the Scotsman. 'But what d'ye know about fichting in the air?'

'I've done a little,' Ginger told him.

'Ye mean—ye're a pilot?'

'I am.'

'Then what are ye doing in the trenches?'

For the first time in two days a thrill of hope shot into Ginger's heart as he saw to what possibilities the

90

chance meeting might lead. 'I only arrived in the trenches by accident,' he declared. 'I want to fly.'

'Ye're not pitching me a tale?' asked the Scotsman suspiciously.

'I've flown pretty nearly everything from single-seater fighters to multi-engined transports and flying-boats,' returned Ginger. 'I'm not bragging. I'm just telling you. I shouldn't say that if it weren't true because you could soon prove me a liar by leading me up to a machine.'

'Yet I find it a wee bit hard to believe, ye ken. Ye look sich a kid.'

'So I may do, but I've been flying for years,' protested Ginger, warming up to his subject as he saw a chance of realizing his ambition. 'There's hardly a country that I haven't flown over—*and* I've done some war flying. Give me a 'plane with a gun on it and I'll soon show you whether or not I can use it.' Ginger was tempted to tell McLannock about Biggles and Algy, but he felt that it might lead to dangerous ground. Naturally, he did not wish to divulge too much now; there would be time for more after he had seen the result of his preliminary overtures.

'Weel, if that's true, I can find a job for ye doon in my flight,' answered the Scotsman.

'The easiest way to settle all doubt would be for you to lend me a machine—wouldn't it?' suggested Ginger earnestly. 'If I couldn't fly, I should be a fool to kill myself by trying, shouldn't I?'

'Ay, that's richt enough,' admitted McLannock. 'But how did ye come to be shoved in the trenches?'

'It was all an accident,' replied Ginger quickly and truthfully. 'It's a long story. Somehow I managed to get shoved into the International Brigade, and found myself up here in the line before I knew what was happening. That wasn't my wish, you may be sure. My trouble is, I can't speak Spanish, so I can't do anything about it. I shouldn't like my sergeant to think I was trying to swing the lead out of the line.'

'No, that's true. Weel, if we can get out o' here I'll hae something to say aboot it. We're short o' machines, but shorter still of pilots, so if ye fly like the way ye charged across to me when I crashed, then losh, mon, I'll reckon the crash on the credit side of the book.'

Ginger, his heart pounding with a new hope, looked at the sky. It was now dark, except where nervous sentries were firing star shells. The firing, too, had died away, except for an occasional fitful splutter of a machine-gun. 'I think we could get into the trench now,' he suggested.

McLannock got stiffly on to his knees and peered cautiously over the rim of the shell-hole.

'Are you hurt?' asked Ginger quickly.

'It's nothin' but a wee bit of a bruise here and there,' was the casual reply. 'I think it's safe to move now, but we'll need to let the fellers in your trench know it's us, or maybe they'll pump some lead at us.'

'Let me go first,' replied Ginger. 'I've got a pal in the trench who will know my voice.' And with that he began crawling quickly towards the trench.

At a distance of about fifteen yards from it he cupped his hands round his mouth and called, 'Fred—hi! Fred!'

A second or two later he saw the little cockney crawling to meet him.

'Strewth! I fort you was scuppered,' said Summers hoarsely.

'We're all right,' Ginger told him. 'Jock's here with me. Go and tell the troops not to fire.'

Summers retraced his steps, and in a little while Ginger heard him calling that it was all right to proceed, so running forward, he jumped down into the trench, McLannock following closely behind him.

They found quite a crowd waiting for them, including the French sergeant and the Spanish commanding officer, with whom the Scotsman at once entered into conversation, with much pointing in the direction of Ginger, who, in the meanwhile, was the subject of much congratulation. Even the French sergeant amazed—not to say embarrassed—him by patting him on the back.

'You've done yourself a bit of good, mate,' whispered Summers in his ear. 'Strewth! not 'arf you ain't.'

'I hope I have,' replied Ginger frankly, but he was thinking on altogether different lines from the cockney.

Presently McLannock came back to him. 'I've just had a word with your C.O.,' he said. 'I think it can be fixed up. I'll be moving off now to the aerodrome. I'll be back in the mornin' maybe. Take care o' yourself till then. By the way, what do they call ye?'

'Ginger.'

'That's fine. I'll be seeing ye in the mornin'. *Adios*, and many thanks for hauling me oot fra' the crash.'

A parting handshake, and Ginger sank limply on to the firestep. 'Gosh! that was a bit of luck,' he murmured.

'No luck abart that, mate,' objected Summers, who had sat down beside him. 'That was guts. I 'ope you'll get something out of it.'

'I hope so, too,' returned Ginger warmly. 'Is there any coffee about? I could do with some.'

Chapter 10
More Shocks for Ginger

When Ginger awoke the following morning he was at once conscious of a feeling amounting almost to elation. He knew that the situation had changed for the better, but could not remember immediately what had happened. Then memory, which had been pent up by several hours of sleep, broke loose, and he flung his blanket aside impatiently at the thought of what the day might bring forth.

Nor was he to be disappointed. After an hour of such anxiety as he had seldom known before, during which time he was obsessed by the fear that he might be killed by a stray bullet before his new plans matured, a messenger arrived to say that he was wanted elsewhere, and that a car was waiting behind the lines to transport him there. In his haste to depart, he nearly forgot something, but he remembered it in time, and asking the messenger to wait, he hurried to the ablution trench where, as he expected, he found Summers washing, whistling through his teeth as he deluged himself with cold water.

He broke off when he saw the expression on Ginger's face. 'Blimey, mate, what's 'appened?' he asked quickly.

'I'm leaving you; at least, I think so,' Ginger told him. 'I believe I'm being transferred to the Air Force.'

'Lummy, ain't it dangerous enough fer yer 'ere?' gasped Summers.

'It isn't that,' replied Ginger. 'I haven't time to explain everything to you now. Maybe we'll meet again—unless you'd care to be an air gunner, if I could wangle it?'

'Me! Not blooming likely,' returned Summers promptly. 'I'll stay where I ain't got so far to fall.'

Ginger smiled and held out his hand. 'O.K. pal,' he said huskily. 'And thanks for giving me a helping hand. Best of luck.'

Summers gripped Ginger's hand. 'Same to you, chum,' he said cheerfully. 'Mind you don't fall out. *Adios.*'

'I'll try not to,' Ginger told him, and then, with something suspiciously like a lump in his throat, he returned to the messenger and followed him as he led the way up a communication trench to the support lines, and then on to the track where the lorry had halted, and where a ramshackle car now waited amongst the various paraphernalia of war. The messenger, who spoke only a few words of English, invited Ginger to get into the car, and then set off down the road at a speed that reawakened in Ginger the fear that he might be killed before he reached the aerodrome. However, he bore the ordeal in silence.

An hour's drive brought them to open country, and shortly afterwards Ginger saw unmistakable proof that his destination was at hand—a wind-stocking hanging limply in the still, sun-drenched air. Rounding a corner, the hangars came into view.

The driver pulled up with a jerk in front of a low wooden building, at the door of which a group of men in various degrees of undress, one or two carrying flying kit, were standing. Among them was McLannock, who at once hurried over to the car from which Ginger was now dismounting.

'So ye've arrived in one piece; guid,' was his greeting. 'The boys are just going off on patrol, so ye'll have to wait 'till they come back before I introduce ye. I've told them what ye did yesterday. I've got to be off mysel' verra shortly, so let's see about this flying. I've a machine waiting. As soon as I see that ye know what to do wi' it, we'll fix things up.'

'That suits me,' agreed Ginger, praying that he would not bungle the take-off.

He followed the Scotsman across the brown, hard-baked turf towards the hangars, in which machines of many makes and sizes were standing. Some distance beyond stood a captured Italian twin-engined Caproni bomber which a number of mechanics were examining with interest. He paid little attention to it, for an awful problem suddenly confronted him, a problem demanding a decision of such vital importance that his lips turned dry at the thought of it. Briefly, it was this. Should he, or should he not, abandon Biggles and Algy, and attempt to fly across the frontier into France, whence it would be a comparatively simple matter to reach England? He realized, of course, that without knowing precisely where the aerodrome was situated, such a flight would entail difficulties, but he knew that he must be in Catalonia, so if he flew north he would, sooner or later, assuming that his petrol held out, arrive somewhere in France. So much he was able to work out by visualizing the map of that part of Europe. He knew that the delivery of the letter should be his first consideration; indeed, Biggles had said something to that effect; but he also knew that once out of Spain he would never get back again, in which case he would be helpless to aid Biggles and Algy, whereas now, if he could find them, they might all get away. In the end he decided to compromise. If by the end of three days he had not found them he would seize the first opportunity of flying to France, where he would post the letter, and then try to get back again, accounting for his absence with the best excuse he could invent.

As it happened, he had been exercising his brain unnecessarily, as he was now to discover. A suspicion of this first came into his mind when he saw that the machine which some mechanics were pulling out of the hangar was a two-seater, although the type was unknown to him. Jock's next words confirmed it.

'Ah weel,' he said, cheerfully, 'we'll juist see what ye can do. Get in the front seat; I'll take the back. She's fitted for dual, ye ken.'

'Er—yes,' stammered Ginger, not a little taken aback at this development. He perceived now that the precaution Jock was taking was quite a natural one; his surprise was occasioned by the fact that he had merely taken it for granted that the machine would be a single-seater, because he knew that Jock normally flew one of that type.

The Scotsman did not appear to notice Ginger's temporary embarrassment, but after handing him a flying cap and goggles, he spent a minute or two explaining the instrument panel, which, he said, was a Russian arrangement.

'Anything in the guns?' asked Ginger, noticing two on the engine cowling.

'Ay, bullets,' grinned Jock. 'Ye never know what ye're going to meet in Catalonia; it can be a Boche bomber or an Italian fighter—there's all sorts here. If ye're outclassed, ye juist run for it, ye ken. If ye don't think ye can fly her, better say so now; it may save me knocking ye on the head when we get up.'

'Oh, I can fly her,' protested Ginger confidently, for he saw that the machine was a normal two-seater type, and therefore unlikely to show any peculiar vice. In fact, he was a trifle disappointed, for the machine was clearly an old one. He had hoped for something better, something more up-to-date, such as a high-performance fighter. However, he gave the mechanic the signal to swing the prop, and after allowing the engine a minute or two to warm up, taxied out into position for the take-off.

'I needn't ask ye any more,' announced Jock over the speaking tube. 'I've seen all I need to know.' Which was no doubt true, because taxi-ing on the ground demands as much skill as flying in the air.

'Are you ready?' asked Ginger.

'Away ye go,' was the brief response.

Ginger glanced ahead for a mark on which to fly, and then opening the throttle, took the machine into the air. He held her straight until he was well beyond the aerodrome boundary, and then commenced a steady climbing turn. 'Anything particular you'd like me to do?' he inquired.

'No. If ye can fly, which I can see for mysel', there's an end to it. But I may as well show ye the line while we're up here. Turn to the right. Mark yon square hill on the left; it's a guid landmark for the aerodrome in bad weather as long as ye don't bump into it.'

Still climbing, Ginger turned in the desired direction, noting with practised eyes such landmarks as he knew might be useful. The altimeter, being continental, registered in metres, not feet, but this was not entirely new to him, and he soon became accustomed to it, mentally converting metres into feet.

By the time the River Ebro came into view they were at ten thousand feet, and once more Ginger asked for instructions. He thought the position of the enemy front line had moved, as if there had been a big advance, but he did not trouble to confirm this.

'It's quiet, so ye may as well fly along the line for a bit; the trenches are plain enough to see,' was the reply.

'What about the three machines over on the right?'

Jock gave a startled exclamation. 'Losh, mon, I didna see 'em. They're Fiats. Better get back; we're no match for 'em in this auld pantechnicon.'

Ginger turned instantly, for he had no desire to find himself involved in a dog-fight. But he flew with one eye on the Fiats which, starting with superior altitude, were rapidly overtaking the two-seater. 'They'll catch us,' he announced calmly.

'Ay, so I see,' muttered Jock anxiously. 'Better let me have the machine.'

'Have you got a gun?'

'No.'

'The gun control's on my joystick,' Ginger pointed out. 'I can't use it if you're flying. You'd better leave it to me. I shan't fight unless I have to.'

'A'richt. See what ye can do. 'Twas my own fault for coming so far. Maybe if things get too hot ye'd better spin down out of it.'

Ginger glanced down and saw a terrifying vista of rocky crags, for they were still over mountain country. 'I'd sooner take my chance up here than pile up on that stuff,' he said, at the same time pushing the stick forward for more speed.

'Mebbe you're richt,' came from Jock anxiously.

Ginger, looking back over his shoulder, saw that the three Fiats, now in a loose V formation, were less than half a mile behind and fast closing the gap between them. Watching the enemy machines closely, he flew on, and presently derived a crumb of satisfaction when, at a range of not less than a quarter of a mile, the leading Fiat opened fire. This told Ginger a good deal. He realized that the leader was new to the business, and possibly nervous, or he would not have opened fire at a distance so far outside effective range. Further, if the leader was inexperienced in air fighting, it was reasonable to suppose that his two assistants were no better. It is upon such observations as this that success in air combat depends.

By this time the two-seater was down to six thousand, still racing for home, but with a long way to go. Looking back again, Ginger saw that the Fiats had closed up, and were still gaining; and it was at that moment that the first thrill of resentment surged through him. Until then he would have avoided conflict at almost any cost, for he was—for good reasons—anxious to get back to the aerodrome. But it is not easy to accept blows without retaliating, and when presently a bullet struck the two-seater his irritation became cold anger. A snarl from Jock fostered an idea that was fast taking shape in his mind. His lips tightened, as did his grip on the joystick. He glanced up at the sun, now a blaze of white light in the blue sky, and then jammed the joystick forward for speed.

He heard Jock gasp in dismay, for in such a position they were very vulnerable; but he was flying with his head turned over his shoulder, and the instant he saw the nearest Fiat tracer streaking towards him he dragged the stick back, and then pulled it into his right

100

thigh. The two-seater zoomed up into the sun like a swerving rocket.

Ginger was still watching the Fiats. The manoeuvre had—as he had hoped—taken them by surprise, and they hesitated; unable to look up into the blinding glare of the sun, they were uncertain of the two-seater's position, so being loath to part company, they broke formation and circled, two of them waiting for a move from their leader, or the reappearance of their quarry. This was a normal procedure: Ginger had expected it to happen and had made his manoeuvre with that object in view. The Fiats were where he wanted them. He could see them but they could not see him. His face was rather pale, but a faint smile crossed it as he thrust the stick forward at an angle that sent the machine down like a thunderbolt. One of the Fiats was a little apart from the others, the pilot still circling in obvious indecision. A touch of right rudder brought the nose of Ginger's machine in line with it, but he held his fire. This was his chance, and he had no intention of spoiling it through precipitate action. Not until he was within a hundred feet of it, and had it dead in the centre of his ring sight, did he squeeze the trigger-grip on his joystick.

At such a range there was, of course, only time for a short burst, or a collision was inevitable. But it could hardly fail to be effective. From the manner in which the Fiat's nose jerked up Ginger knew that the pilot had been hit. How badly he did not for the moment know. The other machines were turning towards him, so he dragged the stick back, and, after holding his breath for an instant, when a collision seemed certain, he zoomed back up into the sun. At the top of the zoom he flicked round to meet head-on the other machines if they had followed him.

One glance was enough to reveal the situation. One Fiat was spinning earthward. The other two were flying away, one, nose down, in a panic retreat.

Ginger's gasp of relief was drowned in Jock's yell of triumph.

'Shall I follow them?' shouted Ginger, half wild with exultation.

'No, ye fool,' roared Jock. 'Ye can't catch 'em; they've the legs of us.'

Ginger pushed up his goggles with a trembling hand, for now that the danger was passed reaction at once set in. He looked down for the spinning Fiat. It took him a minute or two to find it. Then he saw it. It was no longer spinning. It had crashed. The country around was strange, and he realized that he was lost. 'Where am I?' he asked through the speaking tube.

'A'richt. I'll take her,' said Jock.

Ginger was quite prepared for him to do so. He took his feet off the rudder-bar and settled himself back in his seat with a feeling of pardonable satisfaction. Jock had asked him if he could fly. He had answered that question in a manner more conclusive than anything he could have said. For the first time for three days he felt like singing.

Jock took the machine home without further incident. Almost before it had stopped running over the dusty turf he had reached over and clapped Ginger on the shoulder. 'Guid boy,' he said delightedly. 'I couldna hae done it better mysel'.'

Ginger smiled a trifle sheepishly.

'Who taught ye to fly like that?' inquired Jock.

'Biggles,' answered Ginger unthinkingly. The word

slipped off his tongue. He regretted it instantly—not that there seemed to be any serious reason why he should.

The broad grin on Jock's face died away instantly. It was replaced by a look of curious inquiry. '*Who* did you say?' he asked in an odd tone of voice.

'Biggles,' repeated Ginger, slowly. There was nothing else he could say.

'*Biggles?*'

'Yes. A friend of mine—my boss really. His proper name is Bigglesworth.'

Jock glanced around. There was something almost furtive in his manner. Then he got back into his seat and taxied quickly to the hangar, where he jumped out and beckoned to Ginger. 'Come over here,' he said, in a voice that made Ginger's heart sink.

Ginger followed him into a small room roughly furnished as an office. Flying kit hung from pegs on the wall, on which, too, was pinned a map showing the trench lines, and small circles which obviously indicated aerodromes. He closed the door behind him.

'What's wrong?' asked Ginger wonderingly, startled by Jock's sudden change of manner, and unable to find any reason for it.

The Scotsman faced him grimly. The corners of his mouth were drawn down. 'And so ye're Mr. Hebblethwaite, na doot?' he asserted harshly.

'Why, yes—that's right,' agreed Ginger. 'What's the matter?'

'I'll show ye what's the matter, ye spyin' rat,' snarled the Scotsman, whipping an automatic out of a drawer and thrusting it into Ginger's stomach. 'Stand still, ye skunk, before I blow ye in halves.'

Ginger felt the blood drain from his face. He stared

103

at the irate Scotsman in horror and alarm. In a moment of time all his plans had been swept away. 'What on earth are you talking about?' he cried, although in his heart he realized that McLannoch had an inkling of the truth.

'Ye low-down sneaking spy,' snarled the Scotsman.

'You're wrong. You're all wrong,' cried Ginger desperately. 'Where did you get that idea from?'

'Never mind where I got it from, but I know ye're a spy. Now deny it.'

'I'm sorry to have to remind you of it, but a few hours ago I risked being shot to get you out of a mess. Just now I shot down a Fiat. Does *that* look like the work of a spy? Should I do that if I was on the other side?'

The Scotsman hesitated. Clearly, this was an angle of argument that he found hard to parry.

'Listen, Jock,' went on Ginger quickly, 'we're both British. I'm going to put my cards on the table. What happens after that is for you to decide. But give me a hearing. I'll tell you how I came to be here—me and Biggles.'

Again a strange expression swept over McLannoch's face. 'This name Biggles reminds me of something,' he said. 'I've got it. There was a mon o' that name in France, in—'

'In two-six-six squadron.'

'Ay, that's right.'

'At Maranique.'

'Ay—that's it.'

'This is the same man.'

'I'll no' believe it.'

'It's true I tell you. Will you let me explain what happened?'

'Ay, ye may as weel.'

'May I sit down?'

'Ay—but keep yer hands on the table.' McLannoch sat down at his desk. Ginger seated himself opposite.

'There are three of us in this,' he began. 'Bigglesworth, Lacey—who was in the same squadron in France—and myself. We've been flying together for some time. A little while ago Biggles had an attack of fever, and the doctor sent him on a cruise. We all went. When we were off the coast of Spain the ship was bombed—'

For nearly half an hour Ginger spoke rapidly, telling the whole story of their adventures from the time the ship was bombed, cutting out trivial incidents, yet omitting nothing of importance. 'Now you know the whole story,' he concluded.

The Scotsman stared at him. 'Ay, and it fits in with what I know mysel',' he said slowly.

'It's the truth,' replied Ginger simply.

'An' I believe ye,' declared McLannoch, putting the pistol back in the drawer. He was still staring at Ginger with a queer look on his face.

'How did you come to hear about the affair?' asked Ginger.

'I read aboot it in the Barcelona paper,' said McLannoch slowly.

'You read about it?'

'Ay—last night. I havna got the paper here or ye could read it yoursel'. It's bad news I have for ye.'

Ginger felt something inside him go cold. 'Bad news?' he whispered.

'Your friends were caught.'

'Yes.' Ginger's fingers were white as they gripped the edge of the table. 'Go on,' he said, in a dry voice.

'They were tried—as spies—by the tribunal.'

'And what happened?' Ginger forced the words through dry lips. He did not recognize his own voice.

'They were sentenced to be shot.'

Ginger's voice became a strangled gasp. 'When?'

'In the morning.'

Chapter 11
Back to Barcelona

Ginger sat staring at McLannoch until the Scotsman moved uncomfortably. Time seemed to stand still. His brain appeared to have become incapable of effort.

'Ay, it's bad, laddie, there's na doot o' that,' murmured McLannoch awkwardly, averting his eyes from Ginger's face.

The words broke the spell. 'Bad?' cried Ginger aghast. 'It's worse than that. It's awful. I must do something.'

'Ye'll ha' to be careful how ye do it, or ye'll join the others,' was the grim reply.

Ginger tried to think calmly, but found it difficult. 'They'll think you're one of the party if they find me here with you,' he said suddenly.

'So I was thinking.'

'I suppose you—ought to give me up.'

'There's no suppose aboot that.'

'Are you going to?'

'No—what d'ye take me for?'

'They wouldn't shoot *you*, anyway.'

'They shoot first in Catalonia these days, and ask questions afterwards.'

'I've got to get to Barcelona,' declared Ginger. 'Do you know where my friends are?'

'They'll be on the *San Christophe*; all the political prisoners go there.'

'Where's that?'

'It's a ship—in the harbour.'

'A ship! Dear Heaven! That makes it harder still.'

'Makes what harder?'

'Rescue.'

'That's a braw proposition, but it's madness.'

'I shall go mad if I don't soon do something,' swore Ginger. 'How far is it to Barcelona?'

'Fifty miles—more or less.'

Ginger threw up his hands helplessly.

'The auld car's juist round the corner.'

'You mean—you'll let me have it?'

'I wouldna stop ye takin' it.'

'You're a sportsman, Jock.'

'Nay—juist a fella fra' Scotland. I'd come wi' ye but the general is comin' round to-night. I've promised to meet him here.'

Ginger glanced through the window and saw the sun was already far down in the west. 'Then I'll get out of your sight before any one sees us together,' he said. 'Before I go I'd like to ask you to do two things.'

'Go ahead.'

'Will you lend me that pistol?'

Without a word McLannoch took the automatic out of the drawer and passed it over.

'Thanks,' said Ginger. He took the fatal letter from his pocket. 'This is the letter I told you about,' he went on. 'It seems likely that I shall fall into Goudini's hands before the night is out. I daren't risk him getting hold of this. Just how much it means to the Foreign Office I don't know, but Frazer, who risked his life to get it, and lost his life trying to deliver it, said it was vital. Will you keep it? If I don't come back here, try to get it through.'

McLannoch put the folded sheet of paper in his

108

wallet, which he returned to his breast pocket. 'It will stay there,' he said quickly. 'If ye don't come back in three days I'll fly across the frontier and deliver it mysel'.'

'If I'm not back inside three days you can bet your life I shan't be coming,' returned Ginger with great emphasis. 'Is there plenty of petrol in the car?'

'Enough to see ye to Barcelona—and back, if necessary.'

'Good.' Ginger held out his hand. 'Thanks, Jock,' he said simply. 'If ever it's my luck to get back to England I'll make it my business to let the Foreign Office know what you did for them to-day.'

'Maybe ye'll ask them to gi' me my licence back,' smiled the Scotsman.

'Why, did they take it away from you?'

'Ay—for low flying, way up in Glasgae.'

'I'll make a note of that,' answered Ginger.

He started as the door was flung open and a man appeared. He wore the uniform of a légionnaire, with wings on his left breast. His eyes were ringed with heavy lines. In his right hand he swung cap and goggles. 'Sorry, Jock,' he exclaimed, in a broad American accent. 'Who's this?' he went on, indicating Ginger. 'Another candidate for incineration?' He laughed at his own grim joke.

'Ay. Friend o' mine. The lad who pulled me out of the crash yesterday; I told ye aboot it last nicht.'

The American struck Ginger a violent blow between the shoulders. 'Nice work, pal,' he drawled. 'I'll be seeing you.' With that, and a cheerful nod, he went out again.

'One of my lads,' explained Jock. 'American. Name's

Cy Harkwell. As guid as they make 'em. Ye can bet on him if ye're in a jam.'

'I'll remember it,' promised Ginger. 'Now I'll get along, if you don't mind.'

'I'll see ye off the premises, in case of trouble,' said Jock, picking up his cap.

Together they walked to where the car was standing—the same that had been sent to fetch Ginger from the trenches. It was, he now saw, an old Renault saloon.

'How are you going to get your car back if I don't come back?' asked Ginger, prompted by a twinge of conscience.

'It doesn't matter aboot the car,' replied Jock carelessly. 'Leave it by the Columbus statue, which is as close to the *San Christophe* as ye'll get.'

Ginger looked up. 'Can you actually see the *San Christophe* from there?'

'Ay. She's a black-painted two-funnelled tramp. She lies in the central harbour, a hundred yards, more or less, in the direction Columbus is looking.'

'Thanks. It's useful to know that. You'll find the car there, I hope, if anything goes wrong.'

'Guid enough. *Adios*, and the best of luck.' Jock held out his hand.

Ginger held it firmly in his own for a second; then settling himself behind the wheel, he slipped in the clutch.

'Keep straight; the road goes through to Barcelona,' called Jock.

Ginger waved good-bye, and sped down the long white road between distant hills now softly purple in the evening light. It would be dark, he reflected, by the time he reached Barcelona, so the risk of recognition was small. Just what he was going to do when he got there he did not know. He had not thought as far ahead as that. He would try to devise some plan during the journey.

But in this he failed dismally. The word Barcelona beat through his brain like a funeral toll. As a boy he had used the word many times, always with the same association. Nuts. Barcelona nuts. He had eaten thousands, not having the remotest idea of where Barcelona was. Now, with faint surprise, he recalled that he had not seen a single nut, much less a nut tree, since he arrived in the great Spanish seaport. Where the nuts came from, then, appeared to be a mystery—a mystery that was likely to remain such as far as he was concerned, for he had more pressing business to attend to.

As he neared the city signs of the war became more evident: marching men, lorries, guns, wagons, and the like. He paid little heed to them, beyond taking care to avoid a collision, which in the circumstances was the very last thing he wanted. As the light waned, so did his spirits. The shock of Jock's revelation had rather overwhelmed him, but as time passed, and his brain returned to normal, he saw the situation in its true light, and he was appalled. Yet he had, he perceived, one card which, if played properly, might prove to be a trump. The letter. Goudini wanted it. Wanted it badly. If it was worth more to him than the lives of the two prisoners, then it might be possible to strike a bargain. He perceived what the end of such a bargain might involve, and he shrank from reaching a definite decision in the matter. Would he be justified in handing the letter, vital to his own country's interests (of that he had no doubt) to a potential enemy in order to save the lives of his best friends, friends who meant more to

111

him than the rest of the world? Either way the remorse would be dreadful; he could see that clearly. So the more he contemplated the sacrifice which such a bargain would inevitably entail—his country on one hand or his friends on the other—the more he quailed before it. But he could see no other way out. But before taking any irrevocable step, he would, he decided, look at the ship.

It was dark by the time he had passed through the suburbs and entered the city proper. He did not know the way to the harbour, but he thought that if he kept to the main streets he would sooner or later come upon it. And in this he was correct. From some distance away he saw the high figure of the great discoverer, gazing for ever towards the continent he had risked so much to find, and made his way slowly towards it.

Parking the car near the foot of the column, he got out and stared across the black water of the harbour at the silhouette of a two-funnelled ship, moored where, from Jock's description, he expected to see it. It was about a hundred yards from the shore. Lights shone on the deck, and one or two portholes were illuminated. That was all he could see. Nor did there appear to be the slightest hope of learning more. But as he stood on the concrete quay, wondering—vaguely, it may be admitted—what he could do, he saw a dinghy leave the side of the ship and move swiftly across the water to some steps not far away. The sound of softly spoken Spanish reached his ears, so, purely as a precautionary measure, he stepped into the black shade of a bomb-shattered bus shelter, or something of the sort. He was not sure what it was, and was not sufficiently concerned to find out.

The boat disappeared from sight under the high wall

of the quay, and he was prepared to dismiss the matter from his mind. There had been only three men in it, so it was impossible that Biggles and Algy should be amongst them.

He had turned his attention again to the ship when a sound reached his ears that stopped his heart beating—or so it seemed. He held his breath. The loose, wheezing cough was unmistakable. Shrinking back farther into his refuge, he saw two men walking slowly along the edge of the quay, evidently two of the three who had been in the dinghy. The other, he thought, was probably the boatman. One glance was all he needed to comfirm what, really, he already knew. Goudini was there, a black portfolio under his arm. His dwarf, mis-shapen form was unmistakable. The two were making their way slowly towards a car that stood at the foot of the Columbus column, on the side farthest from where Ginger had left his.

Ginger stood quite still, although his brain raced. He watched the pair as, having neared the car, they stood for some minutes in earnest conversation. Then, abruptly, the unknown man raised his hat and walked quickly away. Goudini, his head bent in thought, moved slowly towards the car with the obvious intention of entering it.

Ginger strode quickly over the paving-stones towards him. What he was going to say, or even what he was going to do, he did not know. He had had no time to think about it. He had simply acted on the spur of the moment, believing that the opportunity was heaven-sent.

Goudini, hearing footsteps, glanced over his shoulder, but seeing only a lone légionnaire, from whom, presumably, he had nothing to fear, he turned

113

back to the car. His hand closed over the handle of the door. It swung open. He put his foot on the running-board.

Ginger pressed the muzzle of the automatic into the small of his back. 'Just a moment, Señor Goudini, if you don't mind,' he said softly.

Chapter 12

A Desperate Expedient

Ginger felt Goudini stiffen. Slowly the Spaniard turned his head and looked over his shoulder. His eyes gleamed under heavy lids when he saw who it was, but his expression did not alter.

'Ah,' he said softly, 'so you have come back.'

'Get in the car,' returned Ginger curtly. 'I want to talk to you.'

The Spaniard hesitated, his eyes flashing round the square adjoining the quay.

'Señor Goudini,' went on Ginger, 'at the first sign of trouble I shall shoot you, so whatever happens afterwards will afford you little satisfaction. But don't misunderstand me. I do not want to kill you. You mean nothing to me. Nothing at all. Neither does your country. I know nothing about your war. I don't want to know anything about it, but I hope the side wins that represents the majority of true Spaniards. You have made the quarrel that exists between us. You are holding my friends prisoners. They are my sole concern. To obtain their release I would shoot you and a hundred men like you, so be careful.' Ginger put out his hand and tapped the Spaniard's pockets. From one he took a revolver, and put it in his own. 'Now get in the car,' he said.

The Spaniard shrugged his shoulders, coughed painfully, and then got into the nearest seat.

Ginger's heart was palpitating violently and his brain

raced as he tried to think of a way to turn his present advantage to good account. Far from there being any fixed plan in his mind, he was utterly at a loss to know what to do next. For a few seconds he contemplated the possibility of forcing Goudini, at the muzzle of his gun, back to the ship, and there ordering the release of the prisoners. He had seen that sort of thing done on the films, one man obediently obeying the orders of another who walks beside him with a revolver in his pocket, the muzzle prodding the victim's ribs. But he realized now that while this may look all very simple from the comfortable seat of a theatre, in actual fact the chances of success were so remote that he dismissed it from his mind as utterly impracticable.

'Well?' said Goudini suggestively.

Ginger started. He realized that he could not sit where he was indefinitely. He would have to do something; yet after his dramatic coup, to step out of the car and allow Goudini to drive away was an anti-climax not to be considered. In sheer desperation he slipped in the clutch, and, without knowing where he was going, started off across the square and down the first street he came to. And he drove fast, perceiving that in such circumstances Goudini would not be able to make active protest without risk of upsetting the car.

Straight through the city he tore; the shops gave way to villas as he entered a residential quarter, and the villas to open country. The moon was full, and the road lay like a broad grey ribbon before him, climbing in wide curves into the mountains that frown upon the city from behind.

The road was practically free from traffic; apart from an occasional pedestrian or cyclist, and yellow lights that gleamed from the windows of isolated houses set

116

back among the hills, the country-side was deserted. Ginger, holding the wheel in one hand and the automatic in the other, raced on. The drive was at least giving him time to think, and he racked his brains as never before for a solution to the knotty problem confronting him.

He could think of only one thing that promised hope of success; even that was vague, and at its best was little more than a forlorn hope. He studied the road ahead through the windscreen. On both sides rows of vines stretched away as far as he could see. The only building in sight was a dilapidated stone hut some distance from the road, used perhaps by the workmen during the grape harvest. He decided that it would suit his purpose. He might find a better place farther on; on the other hand, he might reach a district where conditions were less favourable. Abruptly he pulled the car to a stop on the side of the road.

'Now we can talk without fear of interruption,' he said harshly.

He found the light switch and flashed it on. Then he turned to Goudini, who was regarding him with a sardonic smile, holding his portfolio on his knees.

Now Ginger's plan involved the use of pen and paper, and as far as he could see, the portfolio alone offered possibilities in this direction. He himself had neither pen nor paper. If the portfolio turned out to be empty—well, he would have to think of some other plan. But he was hopeful that this would not be necessary. He had seen such portfolios before; in fact, Biggles had one, and in it there were compartments for useful things such as writing paper, visiting cards, envelopes, and the like.

'Give me that bag,' ordered Ginger.

117

Goudini's answer was to hold it more tightly.

'Do what I tell you, or I'll shoot you out of hand,' snarled Ginger.

Whether or not he would have carried out his dire threat is open to question; but in his state of mind he was fully convinced that he would, which may have expressed itself in his tone of voice. Goudini evidently thought he was capable of it, for he passed the portfolio over.

Ginger soon discovered that it was locked. 'Give me the key,' he grated; 'wasting time won't help you.

Goudini felt in his wasitcoat pocket, took out the key and handed it over. 'There is nothing likely to interest you in it,' he said, obviously referring to the bag.

'I'll find out for myself,' returned Ginger.

There was a sheaf of documents, but he was not concerned with them. In any case, he knew that any written matter would be in Spanish, and therefore unintelligible to him. He repressed the grunt of satisfaction that rose to his lips as he found what he was looking for in one of the narrow compartments—a few spare sheets of writing paper. The fact that they bore a printed heading was all the better for his purpose. He took out the paper, laid it on the portfolio, and passed it to Goudini.

'Write what I tell you,' he said. 'Write in Spanish, of course.'

'What do you think to do?'

'You are going to do it, not me. You are going to write an order for the release of my friends.'

Goudini laughed shortly. 'Do you think that the commandant would be such a fool as to hand two prisoners over just like that?'

118

Ginger pursed his lips. 'Very well; say they are to accompany me to your office.'

'You think he would not remark that it was strange for two prisoners to be given to an escort of one man — yes?'

Ginger groped in his mind for an alternative. He realized that Goudini was right. 'Then you shall write a letter authorizing me, as an interpreter, to visit the English prisoners for the purpose of interrogation,' he said.

'Has it occurred to you that, since you cannot read Spanish, the message that I write might differ considerably from the one you dictate?' Goudini's manner was one of slightly amused tolerance. It was apparent that he thought not all the advantages of the strange game they were playing lay with Ginger.

'The message you write will be the one I dictate,' returned Ginger grimly. 'To prevent — er — accidents, perhaps I had better make my intention plain to you. I shall, of course, take the letter straight to the commandant of the prison ship, hoping — as you will have supposed — that I shall then be able to find a way of releasing my friends, by which time my success will be as important a matter to you as to me; for before I go I shall tie you securely and leave you in some place I have yet to decide upon — probably the stone farm building over on the left. This tying up business is as distasteful to me as it will be to you; it is sort of cheap drama; but to be quite frank, I can't think of any alternative. If my mission is successful I shall at once come back here to release you. I need not enlarge upon the consequences of failure to achieve my object; you will probably die a miserable death from hunger and thirst. Now you know just what I mean when I say

119

that your prayers should be for my success. In your own interest you will give me all the help you can. Now write the letter. Word it as you like, but the gist of it will be that I am to be given access to my friends.'

'And if I refuse?'

'I shall shoot you here and now. Your disappearance will probably help my cause by giving your pet sleuths something else to think about than me and my friends. Go ahead and write.'

Goudini looked at Ginger curiously for a moment, and then wrote rapidly on the top sheet of paper. He signed it with a flourish, and handed it to Ginger.

'Address the envelope and mark it "Personal" and "Urgent",' ordered Ginger.

Goudini obeyed.

Ginger laid the two documents on the back seat of the car for the ink to dry. 'Now get out,' he said.

The sardonic smile still played about the corners of the Spaniard's lips as he opened the door on his side of the car, and got out on to the roadside. Ginger followed.

Now apart from the fact that the action of getting out of a motor-car demands a certain amount of attention, as well as some minor contortions of the body, it may have been that Ginger's original suspicious alertness had been somewhat dulled by Goudini's submissive attitude. However that may be, Ginger was quite unprepared for what happened as he slid out of the car, feet first, in the most natural manner. He still held the automatic in his right hand, but at the moment of his emergence it was resting against the inside of the door frame to steady his descent. It was at that moment that Goudini leapt at him, his dwarf, misshapen body moving at a speed that could not have been suspected.

Ginger saw the gleam of moonlight on steel as Goudi-ni's arm swung upward and down in a vicious half circle. Instinctively he flung up his arm to shield his body—his right arm, that being the side from which Goudini had launched his attack. The immediate result of this was that, losing his support, he fell backwards; which was, actually, to his advantage, since the fall was away from the knife. The weapon, therefore, swept short of his body, but struck his forearm.

Ginger did not consciously pull the trigger of the automatic. His entire faculties were concentrated on avoiding the knife. His grip may have tightened on the pistol instinctively, or the blow may have been responsible for his fingers tightening convulsively. Anyway, the pistol exploded. Ginger went over back-wards. He twisted sideways as he fell, and was on his feet again in an instant, crouching, panting, staring at Goudini, who lay moaning feebly on the white road. As he watched, the moans died away to silence.

Ginger felt a wave of nausea sweep over him. The moonlight faded to a swimming blackness, and for a horrible moment he thought he was going to faint. He nearly did. But he managed to reach the running board of the car, and squatting down on it, allowed his head to sag between his knees—which was the best thing he could have done.

The nausea passed. He sat up, but he still felt weak and shaky. His legs had no strength in them, and he knew that he was unable to stand. He felt something hot running over his hand; looking down, he saw blood dripping from his fingers, forming a little pool, black in the moonlight in the dust of the road. He looked at Goudini. He was lying quite still, his face buried in his arms. Pulling himself to his feet by hanging on to the

121

side of the car, Ginger stood for a moment fighting another wave of sickness, and then went over to him. He turned him over. The body was horribly limp. The Spaniard's face was ashen. Ginger kicked the knife aside and, bending down, felt for the fallen man's heart. It was beating. 'Thank God, he isn't dead,' thought Ginger. 'Poor devil, I ought to do something for him. I can't leave him here to die.'

The shock having passed, his strength began to come back quickly. He took off his coat and examined the wound in his arm. It was not very long, but it was deep, and bleeding copiously. He knew that he would have to stop it.

It took him some time to adjust a bandage, using Goudini's handkerchief for a wad, and his own to tie it on. With no medical appliances available, there was nothing more he could do. He picked up the automatic, which still lay where it had fallen, and put it in his pocket. Then he returned to the Spaniard with the intention of lifting him into the car. What he was going to do with him he did not know. He only knew that he could not leave him there. Then, to his consternation, he found that single-handed he could not lift the limp body.

He stood staring down at the white face. He was on the point of giving up altogether. He felt sick and weak, and was deadly tired. He wanted to creep away somewhere and sleep, and then awake from what was becoming more and more like one of those nightmares that seem to go on indefinitely without leading anywhere. The situation was getting beyond him.

He was still staring at the fallen man when the jangle of a bell made him look up in the direction whence it came. Coming towards him over the brow of a hill a few hundred yards away was a line of mules with men walking beside them.

Ginger scrambled into the car in something like a panic. To stay was to be accused of murder, or attempted murder, by men whose language he could not speak; he would not be able to explain—not that explanation was likely to benefit him. The new-comers would have to look after Goudini. There was nothing else for it. Not without difficulty, for the road was narrow, he managed to turn the car. Another moment and he was tearing back towards Barcelona.

Chapter 13
A Memorable Night

Ginger never forgot that drive. His arm ached unmercifully; his eyes burned in their sockets as if he were in a fever; he was racked by fears arising from the uncertainty of his plans, and anxiety for Biggles. But he had passed the stage of being excited. He was calm, and his movements were made with the cold deliberation of something not far from despair. True, he had the letter Goudini had written: it was the one ray of hope in an inky sky; but he did not attempt to deceive himself as to just how feeble that ray was. But of one thing he was certain: either he would effect the rescue or die with the others; in short, he had arrived at a condition of desperation where he was prepared to do anything, regardless of consequences, for—as he reflected, gloomily—whatever happened, things could hardly be worse than they were already.

The city was silent and deserted when he reached it, for the hour was long after midnight. He drove straight down to the harbour where, somewhat to his surprise, Jock's car was still standing just as he had left it. He did not know why he was surprised; there was no particular reason why any one should move the car; yet things had gone so awry during the last few days that he fully expected to find it gone.

He parked Goudini's car beside the other and, with the letter in his pocket, walked briskly to the edge of the quay. No purpose would be served by delay. Indeed, he

124

realized that if Goudini recovered consciousness there was a chance that he might start a hue and cry either by sending a messenger or by using a distant telephone. The prison ship lay as she had been when he last saw her; there were fewer lights on board, that was the only difference. The first question was how to get to her. There was no small boat available where he stood, so, remembering the dinghy, he walked along the edge of the quay towards the place where Goudini had come ashore. He was not surprised to find steps leading down to the water; and at the bottom of them the dinghy floated on the black water. He looked about for the boatman, but he was nowhere to be seen. Ginger had rather hoped that he would be there; it would have given his visit a more authentic touch. However, he had to do without him.

He got into the boat, cast off, and rowed as quickly as his wounded arm would allow towards where the black hull of the prison ship rose high against the starry sky. The last thing he wanted was that his approach should appear furtive. He could not hope to get on board without being seen, so his only chance lay in sheer open-handed bluff. At a distance of forty or fifty yards he let out a hail, which was answered immediately from the deck; somebody called out something in Spanish, but as he did not understand he took no notice, but went on rowing towards his objective.

He had almost reached the ship's side when a small searchlight stabbed the darkness, flooding him and the dinghy with blinding white light. It lasted only for a few moments, at the end of which time the operator, thinking probably that there was nothing to fear from a single man, switched the light out.

Ginger, seeing that the dinghy now had enough way

on her to reach the ship, pulled his oars in, and looking round, saw, as he expected, a companion-way leading from the deck down to a mooring raft. Unhurriedly he made the dinghy fast, and then walked evenly up the steps to the deck, where he was halted by two sentries with rifles and bayonets fixed.

'Speak English?' inquired Ginger as he took Goudini's letter from his pocket.

'English—*no comprendo*,' replied one of the men.

The other took the letter and held it near a light so that he could read the address. He said something to his companion, and leaving his rifle leaning against the bulwark, walked away down the deck.

Ginger affected a yawn, purely for effect. He was quite cool, although he realized that if Goudini had written anything but what he, Ginger, had dictated, then he was spending his last night on earth. The thought did not worry him unduly. He was past caring about himself. If he was arrested he would at least be able to lie down and sleep.

The sentry, who, like most Spanish sentries, appeared to take his duties easily, offered him a cigarette.

'*Légionnaire—si?*' smiled the sentry, tapping Ginger's uniform.

Ginger nodded. '*Si*,' he replied, stiffening a little in spite of himself as he heard the footsteps of the other sentry returning along the deck. A bunch of keys jangled in his hand.

He tapped Ginger on the shoulder, and, picking up his rifle, beckoned him to follow.

Ginger followed his escort down the deck. His heart was beginning to thump now at the prospect of success. He felt that the sentry would not treat him with such indifference if the letter had aroused suspicion. So he followed his guide down a companion-way and along a narrow corridor with doors on either side— doors which normally would have given access to the ship's state-rooms. On each door a number had been crudely written in red chalk.

The sentry stopped before the one numbered fourteen, put the key in the lock, and pushed the door open. The room was in darkness. The sentry stepped across the threshold, and reaching up with his hand, switched on an electric light. Then he stood aside. Ginger stepped forward.

Biggles and Algy, still in légionnaire uniforms, had both been lying down on rough mattresses on the floor. Now they were resting on their elbows, looking towards the door as if seeking the cause of the intrusion. Both stared speechlessly at Ginger.

'Go steady,' snapped Ginger. 'The sentry doesn't speak English, but don't let him see you know me. He thinks I've come to interrogate you. I'm trying to get you out.'

But as he spoke Ginger's heart had gone down into his boots, for he saw that both the prisoners were handcuffed to a chain fastened to the wall. This was something he had not reckoned on. However, he kept his head, and playing his role, walked across and stared down at Biggles. Out of the corner of his eye he saw the sentry leaning against the door.

'I didn't reckon on chains; what shall I do?' he snapped at Biggles belligerently, realizing that he would have to make a pretence of asking questions. As he spoke he pointed an accusing finger.

Biggles' answer nearly took Ginger's breath away.

'The key is on the bunch the sentry is holding,' he muttered sullenly.

Ginger drew a deep breath. 'I see,' he said, and then bent down and stared at Biggles' wrists as though there was something remarkable about them. Then, affecting alarm, he looked back at the sentry and beckoned to him to come over. The sentry came quickly. Ginger pointed to Biggles' wrists. The sentry leaned forward. The butt of Ginger's automatic crashed down on the back of his head and he slumped forward with a grunt across Biggles' feet. Ginger darted to the door and closed it quietly. The whole incident had occupied perhaps ten seconds.

By the time Ginger got back to the others Biggles was swiftly going through the keys on the sentry's bunch, seeking the right one. It was typical of him that he wasted no words on thanks or congratulations that might turn out to be premature.

'What's the position outside?' he asked. 'You can tell me while I'm doing this.'

'All quiet,' whispered Ginger. 'One sentry only at the gangway. There's a dinghy below.'

Biggles by this time had found the right key. He laid his shackles aside on the bed and then, working swiftly but quietly, released Algy. They both stood up.

'What's our best plan?' asked Biggles. 'Any idea? You know the layout of the place better than we do.'

'We'll all go to the head of the companion,' answered Ginger. 'You wait there while I go back and stick up the sentry. He knows me by sight, so he won't be alarmed when he sees me. He might be if he saw us all. If there's trouble, then we'll have to fight it out.'

'That suits me,' returned Biggles in a low voice.

Ginger gave him Goudini's revolver, which he still

128

carried in his pocket. Then he crossed over to the door and listened. All was as silent as a tomb. 'Come on,' he whispered.

Algy picked up the unconscious man's rifle. Then in single file they crept noiselessly along the corridor and up to the head of the companion-way. Ginger put out his hand for the others to halt. 'Come when I cough,' he whispered. Then he went on alone.

The sentry did not move when he saw him coming, but went on puffing at his cigarette. He smiled a sleepy greeting, but the expression on his face changed like magic when Ginger, mouth set and eyes glittering, thrust his automatic into his face. 'Don't move,' he hissed.

The sentry may not have understood, but Ginger's expression must have been enough to convey his meaning.

Ginger jerked the rifle from the sentry's hands. Then he coughed. A swift patter across the deck and the others joined him. 'What shall we do with this fellow?' he asked. 'He'll raise the place if we leave him here.'

'Take him with us,' replied Biggles promptly, and taking the matter into his own hands, with the muzzle of his revolver he urged the now terrified sentry down the steps into the dinghy. All was silent on the ship. Algy untied the painter and pushed the dinghy clear. Biggles picked up the oars and under Ginger's guidance rowed towards the quay steps.

'By gosh, we've done it!' whispered Ginger exultantly. He felt that he could have laughed aloud.

'These things either go like clockwork or else they go all to blazes,' grunted Biggles.

Ginger's chuckle made Biggles look at him sharply. 'Are you all right?' he asked.

'Right as rain—except I've had a knife in my arm,' replied Ginger weakly.

'Keep your eyes on him, Algy,' ordered Biggles, redoubling his efforts.

They soon reached the steps, and hurrying to the top, Ginger pointed to Jock's car. 'That's ours,' he said.

Biggles whistled softly. 'You have certainly done the job properly,' he said.

They took the sentry with them as far as the car, where they decided that they could do nothing else but let him go, reckoning that by the time he could call assistance they would be some distance away. A yell that floated across the water from the ship told them their escape had been discovered, anyway. So leaving the sentry to make his way back to the ship, they got quickly into the car and started the engine.

Biggles took the wheel. 'Do we go anywhere in particular?' he asked Ginger. 'We've been out of touch with things lately.'

'You bet we do,' Ginger told him. 'Straight up the road ahead of you; then follow my directions.'

He guided the car through the city and the suburbs to the road that led to the aerodrome. 'Now go straight on,' he said. 'We've a long way to go, so you can put your foot down.' And with that Ginger, with a weary sigh, collapsed into Algy's arms.

Some time later he opened his eyes, and then spluttered violently as he clambered into a sitting position. His throat felt as though it had been scalded. Then he saw Biggles in front of him, with a cup in one hand and a bottle in the other. He was still in the car. Algy was supporting him.

'What happened?' he asked.

'You passed out,' smiled Biggles. 'Don't wonder at

130

it either, with that hole in your arm. I knocked up a tavern and bought a bottle of brandy and a few other odd things, including a linen napkin with which I've just bandaged your arm. Feel better?'

Ginger nodded. 'I'm O.K.,' he said. And he really felt better. 'Where are we?'

'Don't ask me,' replied Biggles. 'We are on the road you told us to follow. We stopped to buy the things I just told you about; then we drove on to a quiet spot and brought you round. I avoided staying at the tavern for fear of causing comment.'

Ginger looked out of the car window and saw that it was just beginning to get light. 'How far up the road did you come?' he asked.

'About thirty to thirty-five miles, for a guess.'

'Then we haven't got much farther to go,' declared Ginger.

'Have something to eat?' invited Biggles, indicating four paper parcels which had been torn open to disclose bread, cheese, grapes, and figs.

'Yes, by gosh! I can do with some of that,' replied Ginger with alacrity. He helped himself and the others did likewise.

'What happened to you?' asked Biggles.

'That's a long story,' answered Ginger with his mouth full of bread and cheese. 'I'll tell you all about it presently. What happened, to *you*?'

'We were caught. That's all,' Biggles told him.

'You mean, when you threw me the letter?'

'Yes. It's no use arguing with a score of rifles.'

'And have you been in that ship ever since?'

'We have.'

'I heard you were to be shot.'

'We should just about have been marching out to

the execution deck if you hadn't come along. How did you hear about it? What have you been doing all this time? How the deuce did you get aboard the ship as you did? You might have been Goudini's best friend from the way you behaved.'

Ginger laughed quietly. 'One at a time,' he pleaded. 'I've had a devil of a time, I assure you; but I don't think Goudini, personally, will trouble about us for a bit.'

'Why not?'

'I pretty nearly bumped him off—if not quite—an hour or two ago. It was he who stuck the knife in my arm. My pistol went off and plugged him somewhere— I don't know where. I didn't stop to see.'

'Good Lord!' gasped Biggles. 'But Frazer's letter? I saw you catch it. You've still got it?'

'As a matter of fact, I haven't.'

'You haven't! Where is it?'

'Jock McLannoch has got it.'

'Who the deuce is he?'

'A Scotch pilot fighting for the Republicans.'

'But how—?'

'I'd better tell you the whole story, then you will know everything and understand how the situation stands now,' interrupted Ginger. 'Otherwise one question will only lead to another. I've been pretty busy, believe me.'

And forthwith, while the sky turned from the pink of dawn to the blue of day, he told the story of his adventures from the time he had bolted with the letter in his hand to the rescue from the prison ship.

Biggles and Algy listened in frank amazement.

'My word!' exclaimed Biggles when he had finished. 'You *have* had a time, and no mistake. I think you were wise to hand the letter over to Jock—who sounds like a good scout—but the sooner we relieve him of the responsibility of it the better.'

'I daren't risk bringing it down into the city with me.'

'Quite right. Well, let's get the letter for a start. Then we'll see about getting out of this perishing country as soon as we can. It's getting a bit too hot to hold us.'

'It shouldn't be difficult to get hold of a 'plane at the aerodrome,' opined Ginger. 'There were all sorts there.'

'That's the quickest way,' agreed Biggles. 'I believe there are some British ships in Barcelona harbour, but it would be a shocking risk to go back there. The ordinary frontiers are closed, of course, so an aeroplane seems to be the only way.'

'There is this about it,' offered Ginger; 'Goudini's crowd know nothing about our being able to fly, so they won't be likely to look for us at the aerodrome.'

'Yes, that's all in our favour; it should be all plain sailing now,' returned Biggles as he got back into the driving seat and started the car.

They were soon speeding along the winding road. With the exception of one or two peasants going to work, they saw nobody.

'There's the aerodrome, straight in front of us,' remarked Ginger as the flying-ground came into view. 'We can drive right up, I think. Several people saw me about with Jock; most of them knew I was the chap who pulled him out of the crash, so nobody will be likely to ask us our business. They'll take you for friends of mine.'

Biggles was driving past the hangars towards the living quarters when Ginger suddenly told him to stop.

'That's Cy Harkwell going towards the sheds. He's an American pilot. Jock introduced me to him yesterday. I might as well ask him where Jock is. If he's up at the sheds it's no use our going down to his quarters.'

As he spoke, Ginger got out of the car and hailed the American. 'Hullo, Cy!' he called. 'Do you happen to know where Jock is?'

The American changed his direction and came over to them. 'What did you say?' he drawled.

'Have you seen Jock?'

'Why—you looking for him?'

'Yes.'

The American's face set in hard lines. 'I guess you won't find him here,' he said quietly.

Ginger felt something like a cold hand settle on his heart. 'Why?' he faltered.

Harkwell took a cigarette from a flimsy packet and tapped the end on the back of his hand. 'Jock went down over the other side on a late patrol yesterday— 'bout half an hour after you left,' he drawled.

Chapter 14
Winged Warfare

The silence that followed this staggering announcement was broken by the noise of a machine taking off.

Ginger looked helplessly at Biggles. Biggles looked at Algy.

Ginger moistened his lips and turned back to the American pilot. 'These are friends of mine,' he said, indicating the others with his hand. 'I wanted them to meet Jock. Was there any chance for him? I mean— was he a—flamer*?'

'Not as far as I know. I was with him. A coupla Fiats dropped on us when we were doing a reconnaissance. They got his engine, I reckon. He cracked up amongst the rocks near Ortrovidad village. I got one of the skunks; then a big bunch of Fiats showed up so I pushed along home. There wasn't any time to go down and get a closer view of the crack-up. That's all there was to it. S'long, boys. See you later.' The American strode away towards the hangars.

'That,' murmured Biggles, 'has just about torn it— as they say in the classics. It's a million to one he had the letter in his pocket.'

'I saw him put it in his wallet,' said Ginger miserably. 'It was my fault. I should never have—'

'Don't talk rot,' broke in Biggles. 'Any one in his right mind would have done what you did. You weren't

*Term for an aircraft which has been shot down in flames.

to foresee that this would happen. It's just a bit of bad luck, that's all. Things are being as difficult as they can be. Never mind, the luck is bound to change if we ride it hard enough. But come on, this is no time or place for philosophy; we've got to make up our minds what we are going to do, and waste no time about it— not that we've much choice.'

'Absolutely, old boy; but what the dickens *can* we do?' inquired Algy.

'What about Jock's car?' asked Ginger.

'We'll decide what we'll do with the car when we know what we are going to do ourselves,' replied Biggles. 'At the moment we're on the horns of a dilemma, so the thing to do is—'

'Take the bull by the horns,' suggested Ginger naïvely.

Biggles laughed. 'Smart work, laddie. You've said it. Bull-fighting is the national sport in Spain, so this is where we shall have to—'

'Butt in on it,' grinned Ginger.

'You certainly know all the answers,' declared Biggles, laughing again. 'But seriously, chaps, we've got to get busy. This is the position as I see it. We can't stay here—not that there would be any sense in staying if we could. The first question that we've got to decide is, do we abandon Frazer's letter altogether and see about getting ourselves home? In that case we can either go back to the docks at Barcelona in the hope of getting on board a British ship—if there is one— or help ourselves to one of those machines I can see over yonder. Since all our lives are now definitely jeopardized, every one ought to have a say in that.'

'It's a rotten thing to simply push off without the letter,' muttered Ginger.

'You're absolutely right there, laddie, but it's a rotten thing to have to go on chasing it,' observed Algy.

'Which means that it is going to be rotten anyway,' put in Biggles.

'Honestly, do you think there is the slightest hope of our ever seeing that letter again?' asked Algy.

'Yes, but I should be deceiving myself, and you, if I pretended that it was more than a thousand to one chance. You say that Jock put the letter in his pocket, Ginger? I think he *would* carry it on him. Very well. It's now somewhere over the other side. If Jock was killed, the letter would either be buried with him, or handed over to General Franco's intelligence people for deciphering. In either of these cases it will have gone for good, and it would be sheer suicide to try to get it back. On the other hand, if Jock wasn't killed, then he will either be in hospital or a prison camp, in which event he might still have the letter in his possession. It doesn't follow that he *has* got it, because it might have been taken from him by his captors. There is, however, a chance that Jock is alive, and that he still has the letter. If that is so, there is just a hope that we may be able to make contact with him and get hold of it again.'

Algy shook his head. 'I don't jib at long shots as a rule, but that all sounds crazy to me. Why, it would mean going into Franco country.'

'Of course; what of it? We should be in less danger there than here. Franco has nothing against us, whereas before to-day is out half Catalonia will be hunting for us.'

'How would you prepare to visit General Franco's domain?' inquired Algy.

'Fly there. There is no other way.'

'And be shot down on the way?'

'Possibly. We shall be shot for certain if we stay here.'

'Three republican soldiers in the uniforms of the International Brigade arriving in Franco country by air are more likely to be handed a bullet apiece than a bouquet.'

'I agree. But the result is by no means a foregone conclusion. We should have to invent a plausible story: say we are sick of the republicans—and that would be true enough, in all conscience. At a pinch we could offer to fight for them—fly for them if necessary. I'd do that if I thought there was a chance of locating Jock when we were off duty. If we got the letter we could then fly home.'

'Do you seriously think they would trust us, International deserters, with an aeroplane?'

'Why shouldn't they?'

'And risk losing a perfectly good machine?'

'There would be no need for them to think that if we, in the first place, made them a present of one. The thing wouldn't be logical.'

'Just what do you mean?'

Biggles pointed to the big Italian Caproni bomber that still stood on the aerodrome some distance away from the other machines. 'That's one of Franco's 'planes,' he said quietly. 'We may be sure that he would be glad to have it back. As far as I can see there is nothing to prevent us taking it—always assuming that it is in order, a matter which we can soon ascertain. That American fellow knows Ginger. He's seen us all here. Several people have. After all, we are in uniform, so there is absolutely no reason why they should suspect our design. True, they might ask us to keep away from the machine, but I fancy the very last thing any one

138

will imagine is that we are going to pinch it and fly it over Franco's lines. Why, if we told them that they'd think we were joking—or else they would think we were mad.'

'They wouldn't be far wrong, either,' growled Algy sarcastically.

'Well, let's make up our minds,' said Biggles, with a gesture of finality. 'It's either that—or France. I'd rather go to France—don't make any mistake about that. But if we did fade out like that, without making any attempt to get the letter, we should feel pretty sick about it for the rest of our lives. May I remind you that Frazer did not hesitate to sacrifice his life on the mere off-chance that we should get the letter through?'

'Oh, I'm not protesting,' murmured Algy. 'But you must admit that chasing this confounded letter is becoming a sort of nightmare. What you say goes for me.'

'How do you feel about it, Ginger?' asked Biggles.

'Oh, let's go after the perishing letter,' replied Ginger carelessly. 'We are so up to the neck in trouble that things can't be any worse.'

Biggles straightened himself. 'Well,' he said quickly, 'let's get on with it. If we stay here we shall only get the jitters. Don't hurry. We'll stroll across quietly, as if we've nothing better to do.'

'Nor have we, if it comes to that,' mused Algy.

Leaving the car where it was, they strolled casually across the parched earth towards the Caproni, which was now deserted, the novelty of it apparently having worn off. A number of mechanics were working on machines nearer the hangars, however, but they took no notice whatever of the three légionnaires.

As they approached, Biggles ran his eyes swiftly over

139

the machine, fully expecting to see some damage which would make their plan impracticable; but although there were some sinister-looking holes through the tail end of the fuselage and the fin, there appeared to be no damage sufficient to put the machine out of commission.

'What about petrol?' asked Ginger.

'It's a modern machine so there ought to be a gauge,' answered Biggles. 'If the tank has been holed it will show empty. We mustn't risk starting up until we have ascertained as far as possible that everything is O.K. If once we attract attention to ourselves we might be asked some awkward questions.'

By this time they had reached the big bomber. 'She looks brand new to me,' continued Biggles, taking a cautious glance in the direction of the aerodrome buildings. 'Stay where you are while I have a look round inside.' So saying, he entered the Caproni by the door while the others, affecting the inconsequential manner of casual visitors, strolled round the far side of the fuselage.

'Confound it! Here comes Harkwell,' exclaimed Ginger. He turned to warn Biggles, whom he could now see in the control cabin, but he desisted when he saw that Biggles had already noted the American's approach.

Ginger turned to engage him in conversation as the best way of preventing suspicion. 'Where did this pretty baby come from, Cy,' he inquired cheerfully.

The American did not smile. He looked tired. 'A feller sailed in with it a coupla days ago. Claimed he was fed up with the Franco mob. That sort of thing's always happening. Guess half these dons don't know what side they *do* want to fight on. Say, did I understand from Jock that you had been transferred to the squadron?'

Ginger, wondering what the question might imply, hesitated for a moment. 'Why—yes,' he answered, realizing that denial might lead to more difficult questions.

'O.K., that's swell,' returned the American, who did not appear to be interested in Biggles or Algy—not that there was any reason why he should be, since Ginger had introduced them as friends of his. 'We're short of fellers this morning,' continued Harkwell. 'Lopez has gone sick with toothache and Schnitz has got a touch of dysentery. I'd like you to make up the flight. We're taking off right now. I've taken over the flight now that Jock's gone west,' concluded the American by way of explanation.

'O.K., Cy,' agreed Ginger. 'I'll just see my friends off, if you don't mind.' He spoke in even tones, although this fresh complication had thrown his brain into a whirl. To his infinite relief, Harkwell turned and walked back towards the hangars.

Biggles instantly got out of the machine. 'I heard what he said,' he announced, with his eyes on the retreating American, and the hangars beyond, where five or six single-seater fighters were being lined up. 'I'm afraid it's going to take me a minute or two to get started up,' he went on quickly. 'If you don't go across right away Harkwell will be back to see what the devil's going on here. Then we shall be sunk. It's a pity to have to break up the party, but I don't think any great harm will be done. You go across, Ginger. When the engines are started up, the chances are that with so much noise close at hand they won't notice the Caproni's engines. When you are in the air, break away and follow us.'

'But if I miss you—where are you going to make for?'

'I can't tell you that. I know nothing about the country. Ultimately I want to get to this village where Jock went down—Ortrovidad, Harkwell called it, if I remember rightly.'

'I say, there's a map in Jock's room. I saw it there,' burst out Ginger excitedly. 'If I could get hold of it I could fly to the village and you could follow me.'

Biggles looked worried. 'This is getting an awful mix-up,' he declared. 'Don't forget you'll be in a republican machine—but there's Harkwell calling you. You'd better go. Do the best you can.'

The American was standing by the line of single-seaters, the engines of which were now being started. Ginger ran towards him. 'I shan't be a minute, Cy,' he shouted. 'The country is a bit strange to me yet. I want to get that map out of Jock's room.'

'Don't trouble to fetch that one. I guess you can have mine; I shan't need it,' retorted Harkwell. He climbed up to the cockpit of the machine nearest to him, and then jumped down with a folded map in his hand. 'Here you are,' he continued. 'That's your crate—the one with the yellow wheels. You'll find a cap and goggles in the seat, and a 'chute. That's all the kit you need here; it'll be as hot as hell presently. Stick close; we're liable to run into trouble the place we're going. Don't forget your 'chute—you may need it.'

Ginger nodded. 'O.K., Cy,' he said calmly, but inwardly he was raging at the unlucky chance that was separating him from the others again so soon.

As he walked briskly to the machine that had been allotted to him he looked across at the Caproni, but there was no sign of Biggles and Algy. His own engine had already been started, so he climbed into his seat, adjusted the parachute—more from a desire to appear normal than any other reason—and then put on the cap and goggles. This done, he examined the instrument board and tried the controls. He was relieved to find that there was nothing unusual about them, but he was by no means happy at the thought of taking up a machine which might have tricks about which he knew nothing. However, he had gone too far to draw back, so he looked across at Cy, who was watching him, and waved to show that he was ready.

Instantly the American's machine began to move forward, followed by four others. Ginger slowly opened his throttle and raced after them, his entire interest now concentrated on his immediate task. But if he had any fears they were groundless, for the machine came off easily, and he was soon climbing up into his place in the formation. Not until he was satisfied that he was master of the machine did he dare to relax and risk a glance over his shoulder at the aerodrome. To his intense relief the Caproni was speeding across it, leaving a swirling cloud of dust to mark its passage.

Taking the map from his pocket he unfolded it with his left hand, and holding it on his knees, studied it with as much attention as the situation would permit. Actually, few of the names meant anything to him, but with the aerodrome he had just left marked down, and the trenches, the map did at least give him a broad idea of the local geography. With some difficulty he found Ortrovidad which, as he expected, was not very far over the lines. This brief scrutiny having occupied as much time as the circumstances would permit, he folded up the map, put it into his pocket, and devoted his attention to the two other matters that now most concerned him—his own formation, and the Caproni, which he could still see far away below and behind him; but since the bomber was not climbing, and the single-seaters were, with resultant loss of speed, the distance between them had not altered except in the matter of altitude.

The course on which the single-seaters were flying suited Ginger as well as any other, so he settled down in his seat, prepared to leave his companions and join the Caproni at the first favourable opportunity that presented itself.

Chapter 15
A Tragic Error

With the formation still climbing, Ginger flew on through a cloudless sky. He was sorry the sky was cloudless; it would have suited his purpose much better had there been some clouds about, for they would have provided cover behind which he could have made his departure from the flight unobserved. As things were, one or other of the pilots would be almost certain to see him go, and while this would not necessarily put him in a position of danger, he would have avoided it had he been able to do so.

Watching the Caproni closely, he saw that it was following the formation, although remaining much nearer to the ground, and continued to do so after Harkwell, who was leading the formation, crossed the lines and bored steadily into hostile air. Up to this time he had been flying on a course not far from that which Ginger would have followed had he been alone, but when the American swung round to the left, presumably with the idea of flying parallel with the lines, Ginger knew that the time had come for him to leave, for he was travelling away from his objective.

He did not go immediately. He wanted his departure, if it was noticed, to look accidental rather than deliberate, so he throttled back slowly and allowed his own machine to sink under the formation, where it could not be seen so well. And in that position he continued to lose height. Not until he was about two thousand feet below the others did he swing away and, cutting his engine, dive down towards the Caproni.

It was lower than he thought, but he was not worried on that account. But when, watching the now distant formation, he saw the leader turn suddenly, he experienced a sudden thrill of apprehension. For the first time he realized the danger to the Caproni. Harkwell could have no reason for supposing that it was the machine which had been standing on the aerodrome when he left it. He would take it for an enemy.

Ginger, tense, turned away. He would soon see whether the single-seaters were watching him or the bomber. He was not left long in doubt. He saw Harkwell's nose dip, and with the other four machines following, the American roared down after the Italian bomber.

After a moment's indecision, Ginger, too, opened his engine and raced in the same direction. He did not know what else to do. Nor, for that matter, did he know what he was going to do. The Republican scouts were going to attack the bomber; that was certain. If Algy had a gun on board he might defend the machine. On the other hand he might not. He would hesitate to shoot at the American. Ginger was sure of that. Nor would he, Ginger, dare to use his guns even to defend the Caproni, for the men now plunging down to attack it were to all intents and purposes his friends. At any rate, they regarded him as one of their own side, so to shoot at them would be nothing less than murder.

Sick with horror at the predicament in which he found himself, and furious that he had not made allowances for such a contingency, Ginger went on down. He knew that Biggles was already aware of his danger, for he saw the Caproni swerve away, and put its nose

146

down in a wild dash that would take it farther into Franco country. But Harkwell, who was evidently a doughty fighter, was not to be intimidated by such tactics. Ginger saw tracer bullets stream from his guns.

The Caproni whirled round in a vertical bank and cut under Harkwell's dive so that the bullets went over him, but the next moment the bomber was encircled by the other fighters who had followed their leader down.

Ginger stared aghast. He knew that such a one-sided affair could have but one ending. Had there been open country below, Biggles might have gone down and landed, but underneath lay a wide area of scrub from which protruded gaunt outcrops of grey stone. To attempt to land on such a place would involve risks as great as remaining in the air. True, open fields and vineyards began some distance farther on, but could Biggles reach them? To Ginger, watching in a fever of anxiety, it seemed to be his only chance.

So engrossed was Ginger in this catastrophic dog-fight that he did not once look in any other direction, and this omission might well have terminated the proceedings as far as he was concerned. It was brought to his notice by the harsh chatter of a machine-gun close behind him and the whip-like lash of a bullet striking his machine. With a violent start he kicked his rudder and then looked round, to stare in amazement at a cloud of strange machines, the nationality of which, since they were shooting at him, he had no reason to doubt.

Curiously enough his first feeling was one of relief, for he perceived that if these were Franco planes—and they obviously were—they would protect the Caproni. But when one of them roared at him with its guns streaming flame he realized with an unpleasant shock that the situation had not improved. It had merely changed. It was he now who was being attacked.

He did not hesitate. He decided to fight. That he bore no ill-will against his attackers made no difference. They were shooting at him. They would kill him if they could. They probably would, anyway. But he would not sit still and be shot like a rabbit. If they wanted to fight—well, they could have it.

While these thoughts were racing through his brain Ginger had not been idle. Ability to think and act at the same time is the first essential qualification in air-fighting—so much Biggles had taught him; so while he endeavoured to focus the situation in its new light, he put his machine through a series of evolutions calculated to leave his opponents in considerable doubt as to his next move. Yet foremost in his subconscious mind was the determination not to lose the Caproni. He could no longer see it. For the moment he did not try to. But he did his best to get clear of the pack that was hammering at him in order to ascertain its position.

A burst of bullets ripped through the centre of his top plane with a noise like matchwood being crushed under a steam-roller. Crouching low in his cockpit, he looked over his shoulder and saw a Fiat close on his tail. In the fraction of a second before he could take action to clear himself the Fiat had burst into flames. An instant later he saw the reason. As it plunged downwards Harkwell's machine appeared through the smoke.

As he roared past, the American raised his hand to Ginger. His teeth flashed in a smile of victory. What he clearly did not know was that a Fiat had dropped out of the blue and fastened on his tail. Ginger saw it.

He dragged his joystick back viciously into his thigh, and as his nose whirled round he fired. Out of the corner of his eye he saw the American duck, thinking he was the target, so close were the three machines together. The Fiat zoomed vertically, hung on its threshing propeller, went over on to its back, and then plunged downwards, emitting a streaming cloud of white petrol vapour.

'That's quits,' grunted Ginger, acknowledging Harkwell's wave of thanks. Then he thrust his joystick forward and, foot pressing on rudder-bar, he roared downwards in a wide circle looking for the Caproni. It took him a few seconds to find it. Then he marked it down, some distance away, streaking, nose down, well inside Franco territory. In a flash he was after it, looking back over his shoulder to make sure that he was not being pursued by a Fiat. Well beyond his tail a cloud of machines were still circling in a dog-fight from which neither side would, or could, break away. Ginger was content to leave it at that. If he could get away unremarked, so much the better, he decided, moistening his lips with relief at his escape from such a desperate set-to.

Turning his attention again to the Caproni, he was a little surprised to see it diving as if it were being pursued. 'Here, wait a minute,' muttered Ginger. 'I shall be losing you yet.' With that he pushed the stick forward for every mile of speed his machine was capable of with the intention of catching up with the bomber. He fully expected now that it would ease up and wait for him, but far from that being the case, the Caproni only dived still more steeply, as if determined to increase its lead.

Ginger, puzzled, lost forward speed by deliberately

149

pulling his machine round so that those in the Caproni could see the colour of his wheels, for he knew that they would not have failed to mark which machine he got into on the aerodrome. But still the Caproni raced on with speed unabated.

Ginger frowned. There must be something wrong somewhere, he mused. He glanced above and below but could see no sign of Fiats, or, for that matter, of Republican machines. It was, therefore, with something like irritation that he pushed his joystick forward and roared down in a shrieking power dive. Not until he was far below the Caproni, by which time his speed indicator told him that he was travelling at nearly four hundred miles an hour, did he ease out. As he hoped, the speed gained in the dive was sufficient to take him up alongside the bomber, and very close to it.

What he saw made him catch his breath with a gasp of amazed consternation; it was so utterly unexpected that his hesitation to act instantly was pardonable. There were three men in the Caproni. Two were sitting side by side in the control cabin; he could see them clearly through the side windows. The third was standing up in the rear gun turret.

There could be no mistake, although, for a split second, Ginger's astonishment was such that he doubted the evidence of his eyes. Then inspiration swept over him, and he realized the truth. He had been chasing the wrong machine. Simultaneously he began to turn away, conscious of a new danger. But it was too late. The rear gunner seemed to hunch himself up. His gun swung into view. Jets of orange flame spurted from the muzzle.

Ginger winced as the bullets bored into his engine. He could feel the shock of them. The machine quivered.

Black oil, hot and steaming, sprayed back over him. Then a dreadful roaring noise just behind him made him twist in his seat and look back in affright. What he saw seemed to turn his blood to ice-cold water—the horror that every airman carries deep in his heart, no matter how hard he tries to smother it. Fire! His machine was aflame. His rear tank was spurting smoke and swirling tongues of flame that licked hungrily along the fuselage and wrapped themselves around the tail assembly in an all-consuming embrace. Already the control surfaces were alight, the fabric tearing off in little wisps, exposing the charred framework underneath.

Ginger stared at this sight, paralysed with the horror of it, while a man might have counted three. He thought he was doomed, and decided—as many men have before him—to die suddenly rather than be burnt slowly to death. He flung off his safety-belt, and in doing so discovered that he had completely forgotten—so unaccustomed was he to using one—the parachute. A gasp of relief burst from his ashen lips. Out of the corner of his eyes he saw the Caproni a short distance away—circling—the crew watching. With his left arm over his face to protect it from the heat which he could now feel, he scrambled out on to the port wing, and, as the machine lurched preparatory to its final plunge, he clutched the little brass ring that operated the rip-cord and launched himself into space.

The machine, a flying furnace, roared on past him as he sank easily and smoothly into the void. The wide panorama of the earth beneath appeared to revolve slowly on a vast turntable. He felt his harness tighten as his downward progress was arrested, and looking up, he saw the billowing folds of the parachute mush-

151

room out. Catching his breath, and thinking a mental prayer of thankfulness, he looked about him.

The first thing that caught his eye was the trail of black smoke left in the air by his machine. It was like a huge ostrich plume, dark brown at the top, where the smoke had already begun to disperse, and growing darker as it neared its terrible fount. His eyes reached the machine just in time to see it crash on the pine-covered slope of a hill towards which he himself was falling.

For the first time he took stock of the country below. He was now too low to see any great distance, but it appeared to be all wild and uncultivated, rolling pine-clad hills broken by deep valleys, although in places the hills had been terraced, the level areas thus provided showing the bluey-grey of olive trees. Here and there an isolated dwelling or abandoned ruin gleamed white in the sun. He noted that the ground beyond the hill on which his machine was blazing seemed to level out, and he thought he could just make out a road winding across it, but before he could subject it to a closer scrutiny his attention was attracted by the fast-increasing roar of aero engines. Looking up, he saw the Caproni diving towards him, with what intention he could not think. His curiosity was never satisfied, for the pilot of the bomber, as if fearful of colliding with the spreading silk, zoomed upwards, and although he banked as if intending to come down again, he suddenly abandoned his project for reasons which Ginger readily understood. He had almost reached the ground.

He saw that he would fall on the pine-covered slope, which now appeared to be rushing up to meet him, and he prepared himself for the shock of impact by drawing up his knees and covering his face with his arms. There was a moment of breathless waiting, during which he could hear the drone of the Caproni's engines receding; then, with a violence that alarmed him, he was crashing through the topmost twigs and branches of the pines.

He was groping for his quick release lever when he struck the ground with a force that knocked the breath out of his body. He rolled a little way helplessly, and was then pulled up short by the parachute's shrouds which had become entangled in the tree-tops. For a few seconds he lay still, panting; then, still fighting for breath, he scrambled into a sitting position to survey the situation. Seeing what had happened, he released himself from the parachute, and then, still half dazed with shock, examined himself.

He soon discovered that he had suffered no serious injury. The side had been torn clean out of his tunic. Seeing blood on his shirt, he took the tunic off, and found that the blood was coming from a nasty scratch on his side—cause, presumably, by the end of a broken branch. His face and hands had also been scratched, but the wounds were superficial, so, after wiping them with the sleeve of his tunic, he thought no more about them.

He became aware that he was parched with thirst, and it was with the thought of allaying this that he rose to his feet and prepared to move off. He picked up his tunic, but it was in such a state that it seemed hardly worth putting on. In any case, the noon heat was intense, and he did not need it; so, after transferring the automatic to his hip pocket, he threw it into the bushes and set off slowly up the hill with the object of surveying the landscape from the top, in order to decide which direction to take. 'Not that it makes much difference,' he thought miserably, as the depressing facts of his position began to occur to him.

Chapter 16
In Deep Waters

It was with some trepidation that Biggles and Algy saw Ginger climb into the machine with the yellow wheels.

'I wonder if we've done right to let him go,' muttered Biggles, looking worried.

'We should have had Harkwell back over here if he hadn't gone, that's certain, in which case he might have wondered what we were up to. We *must* get out of Catalonia, and the only way we can do that is by flying out. I think Ginger is able to take care of himself.'

'Well, I hope so; but I wish we could have kept together,' replied Biggles.

'How is she for petrol?' asked Algy.

'The tanks aren't full but there is enough for our purpose.'

'We'll try to start her up. The formation is ticking over, so they'll be off at any moment. We mustn't lose sight of Ginger's machine.'

Biggles was already busy with the self-starter, and, as we already know, he managed to get the engines going just as the formation taxied forward to take off.

Algy got into the seat next to Biggles, watching the mechanics near the hangar, several of whom were staring at the Caproni. One or two began walking towards it.

'Better get her off,' Algy told Biggles. 'People are coming over here to see what's happening.'

'So I see,' murmured Biggles. He did not like taking off without testing the engine revolutions, but there was no time for that. Several mechanics were now running towards the big machine, which began to move forward as Biggles opened the throttle. He paid no further attention to them, but concentrated on getting off the ground. The machine came off easily; he held it straight until he was over the edge of the aerodrome, where he turned, and then began climbing towards the formation which he could still see ahead and far above him.

'It looks as if we're all set for Francoland,' he observed cheerfully, a minute or two later, although finding that if he climbed he began to fall behind the fighters, he levelled out and contented himself with keeping them in sight, knowing that if nothing upset the plan Ginger would join them.

Nothing more was said until Ginger began to drop below the formation. The distance between them was too far for them to identify the actual machine, but they assumed that the pilot of the straggling machine was Ginger—in which assumption they were, as we know, correct.

'Here he comes,' murmured Biggles.

'The others are coming, too,' announced Algy presently.

Biggles bit his lip and looked down to see what sort of ground lay underneath them. 'I'm afraid this is going to be awkward,' he said uneasily.

'If it comes to a dog-fight, nobody will know who is fighting who,' suggested Alby.

'We shall get it in the neck, anyway.'

'Looks like it.'

'We shall have to bolt for it; there's no other way,' declared Biggles.

And he attempted to do so, but the single-seaters, being faster as well as having height of the Caproni, rapidly overtook it.

Algy was the first to spot the Fiats. They were on his side. 'Jumping crocodiles! There's going to be a mess in a minute,' he declared dispassionately. 'What a mix-up!'

'Keep your eyes on Ginger,' ordered Biggles in a hard voice. He was turning to avoid the conflict, if it were possible. As he did so he saw another Caproni underneath them, diving for home. 'It's going to be a mix-up all right,' he remarked grimly. And then it struck him that Ginger would not know which of the two Capronis to follow.

He was trying to work out a plan by which Ginger might identify them when Algy caught his left arm.

'Look out!' yelled Algy. 'They're after us!'

Biggles saw a fighter diving on him, and turned under it. Others roared round them. Then the Fiats came plunging into the mêlée, and that gave him an opportunity of side-slipping out of it.

'That kid'll be killed if he isn't careful,' muttered Algy. 'They're all hard at it, the whole bunch of 'em. I don't know which one is Ginger. I've lost sight of him. Gosh, there goes a flamer!'

Biggles could do nothing except fly on into Franco territory, while Algy kept him informed, as far as he was able to, of the progress of the dog-fight now some distance above them.

'Hello, there's somebody streaking out of it,' cried Algy. 'Yes, it's him. I can see his yellow wheels.'

157

'Is he coming this way?' asked Biggles, craning his neck to see the machine, which was on Algy's side.

'No! He's going like the devil straight into—what on earth is he doing?'

Biggles knew, or at least he guessed. 'There's another Caproni like ours ahead of us,' he said savagely. 'He thinks it's us.' As he spoke he pushed the joystick forward for as much speed as possible, in the hope that Ginger would see them.

But as we know, Ginger's eyes were on the Caproni ahead of him, and as the possibility of its being another machine did not enter his head, it did not occur to him to look behind him. Had he done so he would have seen the second bomber.

Biggles did his best to overtake the yellow-wheeled scout, but the Caproni was slower, and he could not make it do the impossible. He could only watch, still hoping that Ginger would turn. And, watching, they saw the rest of the tragedy. They saw Ginger's swoop that carried him level with the leading Caproni, saw the gunner swing his gun round and take aim, and saw the smoke streak from the single-seater.

'He's afire!' screamed Algy.

Biggles did not answer at once. His face was grey. His eyes never left the single-seater. 'He's going to jump,' he ground out through set teeth. 'I should never have let him go—look! Thank God! He's got a brolly.'

The relief with which they both saw Ginger's parachute open can be better imagined than described. The machine that had fired the shots roared on and was already some distance away when they arrived on the scene. Biggles zoomed at the lonely figure under the parachute, hoping that Ginger might see them, but at the last moment, rather than risk colliding with the silk

158

and so killing all three of them, he pulled his machine clear. He knew the difficulty of flying near a body that is falling vertically.

At that moment Ginger—although he was unaware of it—was only a few yards from the others, but they might have been poles apart for all the hope they had of getting together.

Circling, Biggles and Algy watched Ginger crash into the tree and disappear from sight, although they could still see shreds of parachute silk caught up in the tree-tops.

Biggles' eyes switched to the crashed machine, not very far away. It was still blazing furiously; what was worse, the dry pines and the undergrowth were also on fire, and the flames were spreading rapidly. Ginger had fallen just above, and Biggles saw the tragic possibilities at once.

'If he's been knocked out in the fall he'll be burnt to death,' he said tersely. 'We've got to get to him. We've got to get down—anywhere. But we've got to get down.'

He looked around swiftly, almost frantically, for a place sufficiently free from obstructions to permit a landing being made, but there was no such place within gliding distance. A little to the north the country seemed more open, so he dived towards it. His course took him over the brow of the hill on which Ginger had fallen, and almost at once his questing eyes fell upon a long, narrow piece of ground near a road that wound through the valley beyond. This open space was, in fact, little more than an unusually wide grass verge beside the road, or what would have been grass had the sun not shrivelled it.

159

The heavy bomber at once began to sideslip* towards it. There was no means of ascertaining the direction of the wind, but the tree-tops told Biggles that there was little breeze, if any; not that it would have made any difference if there had been, for the proposed landing-ground was long and narrow, and permitted a landing only in one direction. Biggles levelled out over it. 'Hold tight,' he said grimly, and the next moment the Caproni was bouncing over hard ground that was rougher than it looked from the air. Once, indeed, the machine nearly cartwheeled as a tyre struck a small piece of rock. A smaller machine would have turned over, but the weight of the bomber brought it back to even keel, and it rumbled to a standstill in a cloud of dust.

Algy flung open the door. 'We are three miles from the place where he crashed,' he said. 'We'll have to run.'

Biggles followed him to the ground, and then, looking about him, gave a sharp exclamation that was half way between anger and dismay. Algy, following Biggles' eyes, saw what had caused it. Fringing the more or less level piece of ground on which they had landed was a belt of pines, joined in places by others that connected it to the pine forest covering the hill beyond. From this belt of trees, under which they had evidently been resting, ran soldiers, possibly a hundred or more. Beyond these stood others, too tired to come forward but prepared to watch. There were also tanks, guns, and the usual transport wagons that accompany troops on the march.

'Trust us to land beside a regiment,' said Biggles

* Aircraft moving to one side while maintaining forward flight.

bitterly. 'We can't do anything. I only hope that there is some one among them who can speak English.'

'If we take off our jackets they might think we belong to their own Air Force,' suggested Algy quickly. 'It's one of their machines, don't forget.'

Biggles shook his head. 'Too risky,' he said. 'To conceal our identity makes us spies. They'd shoot us out of hand. No, we've got to face it. In any case, I fancy they've already spotted our uniform.'

The leading troops had halted. There was a shout. Then they ran forward again, calling to each other in tones indicative of excitement. 'Italians,' murmured Algy.

'They are,' agreed Biggles. 'Italians or Spaniards, it won't make much difference,' he added, raising his hands and walking towards an officer who was running forward with the others.

The next moment they were both surrounded by a clamouring crowd. Biggles tried to make himself heard, but it was no use. The officer shouted at his men and the noise subsided somewhat.

'We are English,' said Biggles. 'Do you speak English?'

The officer eyed Biggles suspiciously. 'English,' he repeated, as if he did not understand the word, or if he did, was at a loss what to make of it.

'Does any one speak English?' shouted Biggles.

Two of the soldiers answered 'Yes.' One pushed his way to the front. 'I was a waiter in London,' he announced in a tone of voice suggesting that he was proud of his accomplishment.

'Then tell your officer that an aeroplane has crashed over there. It is on fire. The pilot may be burned to

161

death.' Biggles pointed to a cloud of white smoke that rose high into the air from behind the brow of the hill.

The man saluted the officer and spoke rapidly. It was evident that his translation had been correct, for the officer rapped out an order at which several of the men broke away and started running towards the hill. This done, he spoke again, whereupon rude hands were laid upon the prisoners, and such things as they possessed were taken from their pockets.

'Why are you flying in one of our aeroplanes?' demanded the officer, through the interpreter, after this had been done.

'We escaped in it from Barcelona, where we were prisoners,' answered Biggles.

The Italian smiled cynically, and, giving another order, led the way back to the shade of the trees, where he again addressed the prisoners through the interpreter. His manner was curt. 'This matter is not for me,' he said. 'I have sent a message to head-quarters. Meanwhile, you sit here. If you attempt to escape you will be shot.'

There was no question of attempting to escape, for they were surrounded by a surging crowd of curious spectators. So, satisfied that they could do no more for Ginger, they sat down. A soldier better disposed than the rest gave them each a cigarette, which they accepted thankfully. They did not talk, for there was little to be said. They sat and smoked their cigarettes, waiting for what might befall, glancing from time to time in the direction of the hill, hoping to see Ginger coming.

The sun began to sink towards the western hills. The soldiers who had gone to look for Ginger returned, but Ginger was not with them. Shortly afterwards a car came tearing down the road. The officer came back and announced that it had been sent to fetch them. They thanked him, took their places in it, and with four men as escort, set out for an unknown destination.

The drive was shorter than they expected. After about twenty minutes the car entered a large encampment which had been erected round a central building of considerable size and importance. It was at the imposing entrance to this building, which now turned out to be a large private house, that the car stopped. The prisoners were ordered to dismount, after which, accompanied by the escort, they were marched inside, halting before a door on the ground floor. A rap on the door and it was opened from the inside. They were marched in and the door closed behind them.

Apart from the escort, which now lined up against the wall, there were four men in the room, all officers of senior rank. So much was obvious, but to what nationalities they belonged was not so clear. Two were certainly Italian. One, Biggles suspected from his close-cropped hair, was a German. They were grouped around a middle-aged man who sat at a massive writing desk littered with documents. It was he who spoke first.

'Your names?' he demanded in a peremptory voice, speaking in English.

'My name is Bigglesworth. My friend's name is Lacey,' answered Biggles evenly.

'What are you doing here, and why were you flying one of our aeroplanes?' was the next question.

'We landed here because we saw a friend shot down. We were flying one of your machines because it was available, and because we wished to escape from Barcelona.'

'Why was it necessary for you to escape from Barcelona?'

'We were wrongfully imprisoned there.'

A faint smile crossed the face of the questioner. 'And your friend—the one who was shot down—was, I suppose, Mr. Hebblethwaite?'

Biggles started. The question—it was really a statement—took him aback. 'Er—yes. That's correct,' he admitted.

'You were on your way back to England—yes?'

'Yes, it was our intention to get back to England as soon as possible.'

The questioner's face set in hard lines. 'You are three English spies, yes?'

'No.'

'Don't lie.

Biggles flushed. 'I'm not a liar,' he said coldly. 'We are not spies. A week ago we were on the sea. The ship was bombed and—'

'You came ashore at Barcelona,' put in the officer smoothly. 'We know the story, Mr. Bigglesworth.'

Biggles stared. 'You know the story?' he exclaimed incredulously.

The officer picked up a newspaper that was lying on his desk. An item had been boldly boxed round in blue pencil. 'Am I to understand that you do *not* speak Spanish?'

'We do not.'

'Then I will tell you, briefly, what this paragraph is about. The paper, by the way, is the latest issued in Barcelona. It was delivered to us, by air, by our special messenger an hour ago. A week ago a British spy in Rome managed to get possession of a very important document which concerned operations in this theatre

164

of war. As a result, it became necessary for him to go to Barcelona to verify certain facts, and to denounce to the Bolshevik leaders a certain important official. But *we* have an intelligence service too. The official was warned, and the English spy was killed. You know his name? No—you wouldn't. I need not ask you. His name was Frazer—the man who, Mr. Bigglesworth, you met in the *Casa Reposada*. The man who, Mr. Spy, gave you the document to take back to England. But you were arrested. The man who caused your arrest was Señor Goudini—am I right?'

'Quite right.'

'You knew Señor Goudini?'

'Yes.'

'He was deputy chief of the Barcelona secret police.'

'That is what he told me.'

'He was much more than that, Mr. Bigglesworth.'

'I shouldn't be surprised.'

'It might surprise you to know, however, that he was *our* chief agent in Barcelona.'

Biggles stared. 'Yes, that does surprise me,' he confessed.

'So you shot him.'

'Goudini was shot whilst attempting to murder somebody.'

'An English spy.'

'No.'

'Yes!' The officer's face was white. He struck the desk with his fist.

'If he was a double-crossing spy he deserved all he got,' said Biggles icily. Seeing at last how deep were the waters they were in, he abandoned caution, knowing it to be useless.

'Goudini is dead.' The officer pointed to the newspaper.

'I didn't know that, but I shall shed no tears on his account.'

'No? Then perhaps you will shed some on your own account.'

Biggles smiled. 'No, I shan't do that, either,' he answered.

The other's manner changed. 'Does it not alarm you that you have killed our most important agent in Barcelona?'

'Not in the least. Would it have made any difference to us, in this situation, if he had not been killed?'

The officer eyed Biggles with a curious expression. 'You know why you were brought here, of course?'

'For the purpose of interrogation, I presume.'

'Interrogation? Come, Mr. Bigglesworth, surely I have told you more than you have told us.'

'I have nothing to say.'

'I think you have.'

'What is it you want to know?'

The officer rose from his chair and held out his hand. 'Give me the letter,' he said.

Biggles shook his head. 'I'm afraid you are going to be very disappointed,' he said quietly. 'I haven't got it.'

'I will have you searched.'

Biggles opened his hands, palms outwards. 'You will be wasting your time,' he returned. 'Should I adopt a course so futile, as well as prove myself a liar, if the letter was in my possession? I haven't got it. Neither has either of my friends. That you will easily be able to verify.'

'Where is it?'

Biggles shrugged his shoulders. 'If I *could* answer that question I would not. But as it happens, I can't.'

There was silence in the room, a silence broken only by the soft ticking of a clock on the mantelpiece.

The officer drew a deep breath. 'I will give you to-night to think better of your decision,' he said softly. 'But to-morrow my patience will expire—you understand?'

'Perfectly.'

The officer gave some crisp instructions to the escort, who took their places on either side of the prisoners. They were then marched back to the car, and ordered to resume their seats.

'We seem to be doing a lot of travelling,' remarked Algy cheerfully.

'The trouble is, we don't go far enough,' returned Biggles. 'Next time—if there is a next time—I intend to keep going until I get to a country where they don't speak Spanish.'

The car glided forward down the dusty road.

Chapter 17
An Unexpected Meeting

Meanwhile, Ginger had found that it was farther to the top of the hill than he had thought. The heat was intense, and the fragrance of the pines almost over-powering. These factors alone would not have worried him, but he was still feeling more than a little shaken, the after-effects of his last terrifying experience. He was also sick at heart at so soon being separated again from the others. However, he staggered on with frequent rests towards the top of the hill, from where, he thought, he would be able to get a good view of the surrounding country.

It was during one of his brief rests, near the summit, that he heard voices calling to each other. Springing to his feet, by listening intently he could hear the noise of breaking twigs, and other sounds that told him beyond question that a number of people were not very far away, and hurrying towards him—or, more probably, towards the fire, which was now throwing up a mighty pillar of smoke.

He was not particularly alarmed. His state of mind was such that it would have taken a great deal to alarm him. Still, he did not suppose that the people now approaching were soldiers; he imagined, rather, that they were peasants coming to ascertain the cause of the fire. But he would avoid them if he could, he decided, and with this object he made his way to one of the several gnarled old olive trees amongst which he was standing, and pulled himself up into the branches.

At one time or another throughout history hundreds of fugitives have chosen this ready means of evading discovery; but Ginger was not thinking about that. He was watching the brow of the hill. And when, presently, a line of Italian troops came into view, he expressed his opinion of them in muttered invective. His fears that they were searching for him soon passed, however, for they rushed down the hill without so much as a glance in his direction.

He did not linger. Dropping from his perch, he hurried to the top of the hill and surveyed the country-side below. It told him little, if anything, although had he struck the ridge of the hill a little higher up it would have been different, for he would then have seen the Caproni standing by the roadside, surrounded by troops, which would have given him food for thought. As it was, all he could see was a broad valley through which wound a grey ribbon of road. There were one or two isolated houses near it, and it was upon these that he concentrated his attention, for they seemed to offer the only hope of slaking his raging thirst. Where there was a house there must be a water supply, he reasoned, and as he had to drink or die, he selected one of them as his first objective. He chose the nearest—a fair-sized whitewashed villa with a pantiled roof, in the usual Spanish style, which snuggled in a clump of conical cypress trees about a mile away.

It took him some time to reach it, both on account of the nature of the hill-side down which he scrambled, and often stumbled, and the Italian troops who, in twos and threes, appeared over the brow of the hill, on their way back from the fire to wherever they belonged.

When this happened he took cover until they had gone rather than risk being seen. Where they went he neither knew nor cared; he was only concerned with keeping clear of them, and quenching his thirst.

Reaching the foot of the hill, he made his way over level ground, through an area of sparse pines, to the road, striking it at a point about a quarter of a mile from the nearest house. Towards this he now turned, but keeping amongst the trees, parallel with the road, both for concealment and the shade they offered.

Presently he had reason to be glad that he had taken this precaution, for he heard a motor cycle coming down the road. Taking cover behind a tree, he was not surprised to see that it was ridden by a soldier, evidently a dispatch rider; but to his intense chagrin and annoyance, the rider, instead of going right on, stopped outside the very house for which he was making. Leaving the motor cycle on its stand, he disappeared inside.

Ginger crept along until he was nearly opposite, and then sat down to await, with all the patience he could muster, the man's departure. Naturally, he had assumed that it was a private house, and while he was prepared to confront civilians, he was not anxious to come face to face with a soldier, who might remark his tattered appearance, or ask questions which he would have found difficult to answer even if he had been able to speak the language. So he waited, while the sun dropped down the steep slope of the western sky.

Once a lorry filled with soldiers went past. They did not see him. An ambulance came slowly down the road, the driver singing to himself, and disappeared round the next corner, leaving a trail of grey dust hanging over the road. But of the motor cyclist there was no sign.

Ginger fidgeted with impatience, deriving a crumb of comfort from the fact that it might have been worse had the dispatch rider arrived a few minutes later while he was begging a drink.

He had just made up his mind to move on, hoping to come to another house, when he heard a motor-car coming from the direction opposite the one from which the other vehicles had appeared, so he shrank back into the trees to allow it to pass before he moved on. With disinterested eyes he saw it come round the corner, travelling fast. He was not particularly concerned with it. He merely wanted it to pass so that he could go on. Nevertheless, he looked at it. There was nothing else to look at. But as he looked he suddenly grew rigid. His eyes opened wide and his lips parted.

The car swept past, leaving him transfixed, staring, his heart pounding, fingers trembling, thirst forgotten. For in the car sat the last two people on earth whom he expected to see in it—Biggles and Algy.

For a few seconds he stood rooted to the ground in stunned consternation and amazement. Then, prompted by something he did not stop to consider, he made a rush for the motor cycle. It was facing in the opposite direction to the one taken by the car, but he soon altered that. He slammed up the stand, and before he really knew what he was doing, he was tearing down the road through the dust raised by the car. He did not so much as glance behind him.

Far from having any fixed plan in his mind, he had not the remotest idea of what he was going to do, or what he hoped to do. His one concern, as far as he was able to think, was to keep the car in sight so that he would at least know where Biggles and Algy were, for the presence of an escort told him that they were prisoners. How this had come about he could not imagine, but when, presently, he roared past the Caproni standing still beside the road where it had landed, he began to suspect; although whether this was the machine that had shot him down, or the one which had recently been at Barcelona, he had no means of knowing. Nor did he particularly care. The only thing that mattered was that Biggles and Algy were down and had been captured. He himself would rather be with them than wandering about Spain, a fugitive, with little hope of ever finding them.

He could now see the car, about a quarter of a mile ahead. It was slowing down, although for what purpose he could not yet discover, for there was no building that he could see. But presently, as he drew slowly nearer, he perceived the reason; a section of the road was being repaired by a long line of workmen, leaving only a single track through which traffic could pass.

Ginger was really beyond caring what happened, which may have accounted for what happened during the next few minutes. In the first place, he drew so close to the rear of the car that had he raised his voice he could have spoken to Biggles and Algy, who sat staring in front of them. He even smiled wanly as it occurred to him what a shock they would have if they happened to look round. But they did not.

He was still watching them, his machine stationary but with the engine running, with his feet on the ground, when a voice close at hand made him start violently. For the words were said in English, and the voice was strangely familiar.

'Blimey, if it ain't Ginger!'

Ginger swung round, and nearly fell off his machine.

172

It was Fred Summers, saucer-eyed with wonder. 'Great heavens! What on earth are *you* doing here?' he gasped.

Summers winked, and went on shovelling stones. 'The blighters got me in the last push,' he said in a low voice.

Ginger, looking about him, saw soldiers with rifles under their arms standing at intervals, and for the first time grasped the situation. The workers were prisoners of war, working under an armed guard.

At that moment the car moved off. Ginger raced his engine ready to follow. Then madness came upon him. 'Feel like a ride, Fred?' he asked, in a curious high-pitched voice.

'Strewth! Not 'arf!'

Ginger looked along the line and saw that the nearest guard was rolling a cigarette. 'Get aboard,' he said.

Summers dropped his shovel as if it had suddenly become red-hot, and flung himself astride the carrier, clutching Ginger round the waist.

The motor cycle shot forward, raising, as Ginger had reckoned on, a cloud of dust, blotting out everything behind it. Whether any of the prisoners, or the guards, saw what happened, he never knew.

'Where are we 'orf to—Blighty?' yelled Summers in Ginger's ear.

'No,' shouted Ginger. 'My pals are in that car in front. I've got to see where they go.'

'Are they prisoners?'

'Yes.'

'Then they'll be taking 'em to the camp, I reckon,' howled Summers, for the machine was touching sixty miles an hour.

'What camp?'

173

'Prison camp. 'Bout a couple of miles ahead. All the prisoners are there. Jock's there. They shot—'

'*What?*' In his agitation at this unexpected piece of news Ginger nearly went into the ditch. He had forgotten the very existence of Jock McLannoch, and the letter which had been the cause of all their troubles.

'Crikey! Look out! You'll 'ave us 'orf,' yelled Summers.

Ginger, seeing the car not very far ahead, slowed down, and did his best to collect his thoughts, which these new developments had thrown into a state of chaos.

'There's the prison camp, straight ahead,' announced Summers.

Ginger retarded the throttle. The piece of road which they were on was deserted, and pine trees from the slopes above had here and there advanced to the edge of it. He could see what he supposed was the prison camp, an area of barbed wire surrounding some wooden hutments and one or two tents. Just beyond it was a village.

Ginger brought the motor cycle to a stop, and dropped his feet.

'There you are; what did I tell you?' said Summers.

The car had stopped. A moment later it turned, moving slowly, towards the hutments inside the wire.

'Get off,' ordered Ginger.

Summers obliged. 'What are you goin' to do?' he asked.

'Get this motor bike out of sight, for a start.' Ginger began pushing the motor cycle amongst the trees; nor did he stop until he was satisfied that it was well out of sight of the road.

174

'What's the idea?' Summers asked. 'Why not get a bit farther away from that blinkin' compound?'

'Because I want to stay close to it,' returned Ginger, briefly.

'Wot for?'

'My pals are inside.'

'Oh—I see. And you're goin' to git 'em out?'

'That's the scheme.'

'You're daft.'

'I'm afraid you're right, Fred, but it can't be helped. You can have the bike if you like. I've finished with it.'

'Not me. I couldn't ride it, anyhow. I'll stick with you. 'Ow did yer come to be in this jam?'

'I was shot down this afternoon. Don't ask so many questions. Just answer some for a change. What sort of a place is this camp?'

'There's two camps, one fer officers and one fer the others—like me. The officers have got an 'ut; we poor blighters 'ave to lay out in the open. There's wire round the 'ole thing.'

'Do the officers' quarters join up with the men's?'

'Yes. There's only wire in between.'

'Anybody in one could talk to those in the other?'

'Yes—of course.'

'Where's Jock?'

'He's in with the officers. They don't go to work like us poor blighters.'

'Would it be very difficult to get out of that camp?' was Ginger's next question.

'Not if you could bite your way through the wire and cosh the blinkin' sentry on the nut.'

'That's all I want to know,' declared Ginger. 'You must please yourself what you do. On your own, I

175

reckon you've got a poor chance of getting out of the country. With us you might manage it, because once my pals are outside the wire we shall aim to pinch an aeroplane.'

'I'll stick with you,' decided Summers promptly.

'You'll get it in the neck if we're caught,' Ginger warned him.

'I've bin gettin' it in the neck, anyway,' snarled Summers.

Ginger turned to the motor cycle, and taking all the things out of the tool bag, laid them quietly on the ground. There was the usual miscellaneous assortment of articles—pieces of rag, an old plug, spanners, tyre levers, and the rest. But the tool he hoped to find was there, too. It was a pair of strong pliers with an edge for cutting wire. There was also a small file and a heavy wrench. He put the pliers and file in one pocket of his trousers, with his automatic, and the wrench in the other.

'Blimey! If a London cop dropped on you with that little lot he'd—'

'He won't—more's the pity,' interrupted Ginger sadly. 'Nothing would please me better at the moment than to see a line of good old London bobbies. But I'm afraid we shall have to manage without them. Hark! What's this coming—more troops?'

'No. It's the fellers who've bin out working coming back to the compound. We knock off half an hour before dark. They come past here.'

Ginger, alert, thought swiftly. 'By gosh, Fred, I've got it,' he whispered. 'I reckon this prison camp would be harder to break into than to break out of.'

'What abart it? What d'yer want to break in for?'

'I can't get my pals out without getting in to them

176

first, can I, you chump?' demanded Ginger. 'Besides, there's another thing,' he went on; 'I fancy people will be looking for me. They know I'm down; they'll guess it was me who pinched the motor bike; but the last place they'll think of looking for me is in their own perishing prison camp. Come on.' As he finished speaking he darted forward to the edge of the road, but remained concealed behind some bushes.

The prisoners, in a rough column, picks and shovels at the slope, drew level. At intervals on either side marched the guards, rifles at the ready.

Ginger stepped forward and sidled into the ranks, Summers, muttering incoherently, with him. He fell into step. Out of the corner of his eyes he saw one of the guards hurrying forward, peering into the ranks. He took no notice, but he held his breath. The guard said something in Spanish. One of the men answered. What he said Ginger did not know, but it raised a titter of laughter.

The guard muttered something and dropped back into his place.

Ginger nudged his companion and marched on.

Chapter 18
Behind Barbed Wire

Twilight was closing in as Ginger, in the column of war prisoners, marched through the barbed wire gate of the camp, which had been opened by sentries for that purpose.

Looking around with acute interest, for much was likely to depend upon familiarity with these surroundings, he saw at once that the place was, in every sense of the word, a compound. Nothing more or less. An area of perhaps two acres had been enclosed with a closely stranded barbed wire fence about ten feet high; the strands were about six inches apart, and along the top one, at intervals, hung an assortment of bells—sheep bells, mule bells, and the like. He perceived that it would be impossible for any one to climb over the fence without one or more bells jangling. At each of the four corners of the camp a high pole had been erected to carry an electric lamp, with the reflector so adjusted as to throw the light into the camp. Cover there was none. Being summer time and warm, this was a matter of no great importance; the question of what would happen in the winter did not arise, for Ginger knew that it was unlikely that he would be there.

This camp had been pitched on gently rising ground, at the top end of which was another, smaller, fenced-in area, in the centre of which was situated a long hutment built of squared timber with a corrugated iron roof. Two smaller ones were just beyond it, one of which, according to Summers, was a guardhouse, and the other a washing-place.

In the large enclosure there had been, when the column marched into it, some forty or fifty men, dirty, unshaven, in various stages of raggedness. Some were lying, some were sitting, and a few were standing up. Most of these men wore bandages, and Ginger did not need Summers to tell him that they had been wounded. The men who had been out working on the road numbered perhaps a hundred, so with the wounded and unwounded the camp appeared to be fairly full, although when the men gathered into groups there was plenty of space between them.

There were not more than a dozen men in the smaller enclosure, in groups of two or three, or standing alone. Being now free to go where he wished within the compound, it was towards this smaller enclosure Ginger made his way.

'There's Jock, standing by himself near the wire,' said Summers in a low voice. 'Don't be long,' he added, as Ginger hurried forward. 'The grub will be brought in any minute, and if you ain't there you won't get none.'

'Go and grab me some; I can do with it,' Ginger told him, and went on.

As he drew nearer he saw, somewhat to his disappointment, that there was a double fence between the two compounds, the dividing gangway being about a yard wide, probably to allow a sentry to make a complete round. This compound was not floodlit, however, for a reason which Ginger was presently to learn.

He went to the limit of the wire and whistled softly. Jock looked round at once, and then walked slowly

179

down the hill. He quickened his pace when he saw who was waiting for him. 'Losh! if it isn't Ginger,' he exclaimed. 'So they got ye. How was that?'

'I was shot down this morning,' answered Ginger.

'Ye weren't alone, chasing a Caproni, were ye?'

'I was.'

'Then I saw ye over the top o' yon hill. I didna see the finish, but I saw the race. Were ye daft, mon, to come so far ower?'

'Maybe,' replied Ginger. 'But listen, Jock. This is important. Have you still got the letter, or did they take it off you?'

'I've still got it. I remembered it just as I was going to take off, so in case of accidents, having no wish to be shot as a spy, I tucked it in the lining of my coat. It's still there.'

Ginger's heart leapt at this news. 'That's fine,' he declared. 'Now tell me, did you see two new prisoners arrive a few minutes ago?'

'I did.'

'Where are they?'

'In the big hut—locked in, I fancy.'

'Are you all in there together?'

'No. There's a big room for the ordinary prisoners, and some smaller rooms for specials—mostly politicals. There's a corridor runs richt along, but there's always a sentry on duty. Why d'ye ask?'

'Those two are my pals. I've got to get them out.'

'How d'ye reckon to do that?'

Ginger thought swiftly.

'Make haste, noo,' put in Jock. 'They'll be calling us in verra soon.'

'Do you mean—they lock you in at night?'

'Certainly.'

180

'Gosh! That doesn't make it any easier,' muttered Ginger. Then he went on quickly, 'Are there windows in the small rooms?'

'Yes, but they're barred. What are yon lights, I wonder?' Jock pointed to the distant hills. They were winking with small lights.

'Oh, I suppose they're looking for me,' Ginger told him. 'They don't know I'm in here. I got in with the prisoners.'

Jock began laughing, but Ginger cut him off. 'Will you try to get a message to my friends?' he said in a tense, swift voice. 'Tell them to be ready in case I come. Tell them to sing or whistle occasionally, so that I shall know where they are. I've tools in my pocket. Give them this; they may be able to cut through the bars.' Ginger tossed the small file across the gangway.

Jock caught it. 'They'd be a week, with this,' he depressed Ginger by saying.

'How many sentries are on duty at once?' asked Ginger.

'Only one at the hut, but there are others outside.'

'What time does the moon rise?' Ginger had forgotten.

'Aboot an hour or so after sundown, I think.'

'Then I shall be through before then,' declared Ginger. 'One more thing. Does the sentry carry the keys of the rooms?'

'Ay, in case any one wants to go across to the *lavabo*.'

'O.K.', returned Ginger. 'Keep awake—you might hear something. I'll get you out, too, if I can; then we'll pinch a machine and fly home.'

'I think ye're daft. Have ye got a machine?'

'No, but I know where there is one.'

181

Orders were now being shouted from the hut. The lights were switched on.

'I'll hae to be gettin' along, ye ken, or they'll be doon to see what's going on,' said Jock. 'Cheerio, in case I don't see ye again. Or maybe I'll see ye in the morning.' A parting wave, and he turned and walked quickly up the hill towards the hut.

Ginger, deep in thought, made his way slowly down to where all the prisoners in his compound were congregated in one of the corners. He guessed that the food was being served out; and his guess was right, for he saw Summers detach himself from the crowd and come towards him with several pieces of broken bread in his hands.

'There was some soup, but I had nuffin' to carry it in,' he said apologetically.

'That's all right; I'm not very interested in food at the moment. A piece of bread will do me. Is there any water about?'

'There's a tap in the corner—and a wash tub,' Summers told him.

Ginger, eating the plain bread, made his way towards it. By the time he had had a drink and put his head under the tap, which was as near as he could get to a wash, for soap was not provided, it was almost dark. A few stars twinkled in the deep blue vault of the sky, but they were dimmed by the electric arc lamps, which threw an eerie glow over the compound where most of the prisoners, weary after a day's hard work, were settling down for the night. Ginger was glad to see that most of them chose the lower end, which was the part farthest away from the officers' quarters.

He shook the water out of his eyes, and brushed his hair back with his hands. 'Come over here, Fred; I want to talk to you,' he said softly, and leading the way to the top end of the enclosure, sat down midway between the two corner lights, where, of course, their effect was least noticeable. 'You know what I'm going to try to do to-night, don't you?' he went on.

'Yes.'

'Then what you've got to decide is whether you play in with me or whether you keep right out of the way, because if we're caught I expect there will be the devil to pay.'

'That don't take long to settle,' answered Summers, without hesitation. 'I'm with you. What else did yer fink I'd do?'

'Nothing else,' smiled Ginger. 'O.K., then. Now the job we're faced with isn't going to be easy. It may end in bloodshed, because once I start I'm not going back, the reason being that if I fail—well, this opportunity will never occur again. Tell me, when you were taken prisoner were any other fellows taken too—I mean fellows I know—fellows in our particular battalion of the Brigade?'

'Blimey, yes! There were about twenty of us trapped in the same bit of trench. There was Chris Fowler from Liverpool—you remember'im—and Jim 'Arris from Manchester. Then there was Abe Morris—I dunno where 'e came from—and Bob Donovan, the Yankee—'

'All right, that's enough,' interrupted Ginger. 'I just wanted to know if there are any fellows we could trust.'

'Strewth, yer needn't worry about that. That lot'd knock anybody's block off for a packet o' gaspers. What do yer want 'em ter do?'

'I'm not quite sure yet—I was just wondering. You see, I've had quite a bit of this sort of thing before, and it's always best to start with some sort of plan. This is

how I see it so far. We've got to cut the two bottom
strands of this wire; that ought to be enough for us to
wriggle under. Then we've got to do the same thing
the other side of the gangway to get into the officers'
camp. That's certain. There's no other way in. Next,
we've got to get up to the hut. That shouldn't be hard,
because it's dark and the lights don't reach that far.
We then locate my pals—one of them's my boss, really.
I've arranged for that. They're going to whistle or
sing—at least, I hope so. Then we've got to stick up
the guard—or knock him on the head. That's going to
be the hardest part, and that's where I thought the
other fellers might come in. If we could arrange some
sort of row, a distraction, the guards would be bound
to go down to see what's going on, and so give us a
better chance. Follow me?'

"Course I do. I remember one night down the old
Mile End Road—'

'Yes; well, never mind about that now. Wait till we
get there. You go down and ask those fellows if they'll
kick up a row when we give the signal, not before. I'm
going to make a start on this wire.'

'What you say suits me,' declared Summers. He
walked away across the dimly lit compound.

Ginger turned over and, lying flat on his stomach,
began to work on the bottom strand of wire. Progress
was slow. For one thing the wire was tough, and for
another he had to keep a furtive look-out for sentries.
Once he had to stop work and feign sleep as a sentry
walked slowly through the gangway; the soldier
stopped, looked down at him for a moment, and then
walked on.

Ginger gave him a few minutes to get clear and then
resumed his task. His wrists ached; blisters began to

184

form on his fingers, but he stuck to it. Presently he had the satisfaction of hearing the strands of wire part with a soft *whang*. He was struggling with the next when Summers returned.

'The boys'll play up when you say the word,' he announced.

'Splendid,' whispered Ginger. 'Take a turn on this wire, will you? My wrists are giving out. I'll keep cave.' He handed the pliers to Summers, who, possibly because his hands were better suited to the task, made quicker work of the second strand.

Ginger looked around cautiously. He could see sentries under the lights in the distance, but none near. 'Right! Slip across and cut those on the other side,' he whispered. 'You're better at this than I am, but I'll give you a turn if your wrists give out. Keep as flat on the ground as you can; I'll haul you back by the heels if I see any one coming.'

Between them they were best part of half an hour cutting the two strands that would give them access to the officers' enclosure. Ginger, who had finished the job, slid back to the men's compound, where Summers was keeping guard.

'I've been thinking,' he whispered. 'There's no way that I see to give the boys a signal. We shall have to work on a time limit. Go and tell them to start yelling, or fighting—anything they like—in an hour, or as near as they can judge. The bigger row they can kick up, the better.'

Summers was away for about ten minutes. 'That's all fixed,' he said when he came back.

'Then we'll go over,' answered Ginger.

After a careful inspection of their immediate surroundings, they dragged themselves under the two

185

fences, rearranging the ends of the wires as far as they were able, to conceal the fact that they had been cut. Then, keeping flat against the ground, they wormed their way up the slope of the officers' enclosure. It was slow work at first, but once out of the radius of light cast by the arc lamps, they were able to move faster, and Ginger, keeping well away from the hut, headed for the top side of the wired-in area.

'Where are you goin'?' breathed Summers.

'I've got to cut a way out of this pen before we tackle the hut,' Ginger told him in a whisper. 'At present the only way out of the camp is down the gangway, and that would take us under one of the lights. It's dark up at the top, so it would be much better to go that way.'

Summers evidently realized the common sense of this precaution, for he made no answer. Side by side, pausing frequently to listen—for it was too dark for them to see much—they crept on towards the top of the slope, and so reached the wire, where, again, they cut the two lower strands. It took them longer than before on account of the state of their hands, and Ginger was perspiring with impatience and strain by the time the job was done.

'So far, so good,' he announced. 'Now for the hut. We've no time to lose. It must be three-quarters of an hour since you spoke to the boys, and the moon will be up any minute now.'

It was so dark now that they could risk walking a short distance towards the huts, the vague silhouette of which they could see about eighty yards away. As they drew nearer they dropped on to their hands and knees, and from this position made a visual exploration of their objective.

The main hut was about a hundred feet long. One

186

side of it was in darkness, but from the windows on the other side came a soft yellow glow. This, Ginger assumed, came from the narrow corridor which ran the full length of the building—the corridor which was patrolled by a sentry. Facing this lighted side, twenty yards away, was the guardroom. The door was shut, but a bright beam of light from a single window cut through the darkness and made a yellow square on the grass midway between the two huts. The ablution hut was in darkness. So much Ginger saw as he knelt, on the rough turf near the end of the prisoners' hut, just out of reach of any reflected light. How many soldiers there were in the guardroom, or whether they were asleep or awake, he did not know; nor did he know which end of the corridor in the prisoners' hut the sentry would be. He could hear no movement, which did not surprise him; having seen something of Spanish sentries, he imagined that the man would be sitting down, for no Spaniard stands when he can sit.

Ginger crept round to the unlighted side of the hut. There was just enough light for him to see a number of small square windows set in the timber at regular intervals. All were heavily barred, and he realized the truth of Jock's remark when he had said that it would take a week to cut through them with a small file. Behind one of the windows, he knew, were Biggles and Algy, but so far there had been nothing to tell him which one. So he waited; and, presently, as he waited, he heard the sound which he had been hoping to hear. it was the sound of a man singing, quietly, as if to himself.

Ginger, crouching low, made his way quickly along the side of the hut and stopped under the window from which the sound appeared to come. As he stood up the song ended abruptly. He could just make out the vague outlines of two faces behind the glass. Reaching up, he tried the bars, but, as he expected—for the hut was almost new—they were secure. They had been screwed in the outside. With a screwdriver he might have taken them off, but there was no time to think about that now. What did upset him was the fact that the window would not open, and as he dare not risk breaking the glass on account of the noise, he had no means of communicating with those inside. Counting from the end, he noted that the room was number three from the bottom end of the hut. And it was at that moment that a wild yell split the air from the camp below.

Whether the 'boys' had misjudged the time, or whether the hour had gone faster than Ginger had supposed, he did not pause to consider. He had reckoned on another five minutes at least, and for a moment this premature fulfilment of the first part of his plan threw him into a state approaching dismay. For the outcry below did not end with a single yell. The cry was followed immediately by others, and the noise so grew in volume that, in the silence of the night, it sounded as if the camp were being attacked by a tribe of wild Indians.

Ginger whipped out his pistol and grabbed Summers' arm. 'Come on,' he said hoarsely, and ran to the end of the hut, arriving there in time to see the door of the guard-room flung open and the occupants, six in number, emerge. After an excited consultation, they set off down the hill at a run; which was, of course, what Ginger had hoped would happen. Below, in the light of the lamps, he could see other figures running towards the scene of disturbance. He waited for no more, but made a dash for the door of the long hut.

Thereafter things happened in a sort of frenzy of excitement.

Ginger got to the door of the hut just in time to collide violently with a man coming out. He staggered back under the impact, and, in spite of his efforts to keep his balance, he went down with a bump. The man fell back against the wooden wall of the hut. Ginger had only a fleeting glimpse of him, but what he saw suggested that the sentry had been asleep. He was coatless. His hair was tousled. He looked thoroughly startled. But he had remembered to grab his rifle. And this, with alacrity, he now pointed at Ginger, who was scrambling to his feet.

But before he could fire Summers had flung himself at him and twisted his weapon out of his hand. It fell to the ground and the two men fell on top of it. The sentry was shouting, Summers was snarling, and at the noise Ginger's skin turned gooseflesh. He threw himself into the fray, only to whirl back as a boot caught him in the stomach. By the time he was on his feet again the shouting had stopped; he saw that Summers was astride the other, hands round his throat, beating his head on the ground.

'All right! Don't kill him,' gasped Ginger. 'The keys! Get the keys.' Without waiting for Summers to obey, he ran forward and, with considerable difficulty, felt in the sentry's trouser pockets. The keys were not there. He remembered the coat. 'Stay where you are, Fred. Don't let him make a noise,' he croaked, and dashed into the corridor. A lamp was burning near a chair at one end. Over the back of the chair hung a coat. It took Ginger five seconds to reach it and take the keys from the pocket. He counted the doors from the bottom end—one—two—three. 'Are you there, Biggles?' he jerked out as with trembling fingers he tried the key in the keyhole.

Biggles' voice answered from the inside. 'Keep your head, kid,' he said.

Ginger gave a gasp of relief as one of the keys turned the lock, and the door flew open. 'Get outside,' he said.

'What are you going to do?' asked Biggles crisply.

'I'm going to get Jock. He's got the letter. You go and help Summers.' With that Ginger dashed to the door at the end of the corridor. It took him a minute to open it. As the door opened there came a murmur of voices from the darkness inside. 'Jock!—Jock! Where are you? Are you there, Jock?' he cried hoarsely.

'Ay, lad, I'm here,' came the well-remembered voice from close at hand.

'Come on.' Ginger turned and ran down the corridor to the outside door. The uproar below had ceased. The sentry lay still on the ground, Biggles, Algy, and Summers standing over him. Ginger, panting with exertion, took the lead. 'This way,' he said, and ran like a hare towards the place where he had cut the wire. He wriggled under the fence and waited for the others to come through. Another moment and they were all outside the compound.

'Good work, laddie,' said Biggles. 'Which way?'

'Any way as long as we get clear of this place,' said Ginger. 'There's a Caproni standing beside the road about three miles away. We'd better make for it.' He turned to Summers. 'You know this district better than any of us,' he went on quickly. 'You lead the way. Keep clear of lights and the village, and try to get us to the road where I picked you up this afternoon. Can you do it?'

'You bet yer bloomin' boots I can. This way fer

Blighty*,' answered Summers jubilantly, and set off at a trot across the field, just as the rim of the moon appeared above the distant hills.

* Slang: Britain, home

Chapter 19
A Bitter Disappointment

Without further conversation they made their way down an incline diagonally away from the lighted compound, now an indistinct scene of activity, and, still at a steady run, swung round in a wide detour that brought them to the road below the prison camp at a point not far distant from where Ginger had left the motor cycle, the existence of which he notified to Biggles. The result was a pause in the pines by the side of the road.

'I don't think it's any use to us,' decided Biggles, after a moment's reflection. 'Only two could use it, and, in any case, as troops will no doubt be on the watch for it, it would be dangerous even to start it up. This place will buzz as soon as our escape is discovered. It was bad enough before, with parties out looking for Ginger.'

'Ay, that's richt,' agreed Jock.

'You'd better give me that letter,' Biggles told him. 'If the worst comes to the worst I shall have to destroy it. It's our affair, and there is no need for you to get mixed up in it.'

'Ah, weel, as ye say.' Jock dug in the lining of his coat and handed the scrap of paper to Biggles, who put it in his pocket.

'All right,' continued Biggles quietly; 'now let's make for the machine. We'll keep off the road. No noise. If there is trouble we may as well fight it out. If we're caught after what has happened — but we needn't dwell on that. I think everybody knows just how we stand. Let's get on.'

They set off again, now at a brisk walk, conserving their wind and strength for an emergency should it arise. They reached the place where the road was under repair, but a cautious reconnaissance revealed that nobody was about, so they went on, gathering confidence but never relaxing their vigilance as they left the prison camp farther behind them. Motor vehicles came along the road, travelling in one direction or the other, and on these occasions, having plenty of warning, they drew farther into the trees until the danger of being seen was past. Another time they had to remain still for five minutes while a belated pedestrian — for it was now well after midnight, they judged — who turned out to be a peasant, went by. But at last, after a long walk, they drew near to the stretch of road beside which Biggles had landed the Caproni. For some time they had been aware of a red glow ahead, and now, rounding a corner, they saw the cause of it. The forest where Ginger's machine had crashed was still alight. The actual fire was still on the far side of the hill, which stood some distance back from the road, but even so it shed a ruddy light over the landscape. Biggles called a halt.

'There were troops under the trees near the machine when I landed,' he told them. 'I think they were on the march; if so they will be gone by now, but we had better make sure. There's no need for us all to go. Stand fast everybody until I come back.'

Still keeping off the road, Biggles strode forward a distance of about a hundred yards to a spot that commanded a view of the place where he had recently landed. Peering through the trees, he stopped suddenly. Then he went on to the very edge of the open space. His eyes swept over it. Yard by yard they examined the clearing and the edge of the tree beyond. He drew a deep breath and returned quickly to the others.

'The machine's gone,' he said quietly.

Jock fired an explosive curse.

'Swearing won't bring it back,' said Biggles calmly. 'The question is, what do we do next? Incidentally, I couldn't see any troops about; that's one thing to be thankful for.'

'By gosh, this is a blow!' murmured Ginger. 'We've got to get a long way from here by daylight, or we're going to have a thin time.'

'We're going to get a long way, too, don't you worry,' replied Biggles grimly. He turned to McLannoch. 'Jock,' he said, 'you must have flown this bit of country more than once. How far are we from the nearest aerodrome?'

Jock scratched his head. 'Corpidello would be the nearest, I'm thinkin'.'

'How far is that?'

'Aboot ten miles—twelve, mebbe.'

Biggles whistled softly. 'Well,' he said in a resigned voice, 'it's no use moaning. We've got to get there. It's our only chance. If we can't make it by dawn—well, we shall have to hide in the woods and finish the trip to-morrow night. We shall have to hide up during daylight. Let's sit down for a minute. Rushing won't get us there any sooner; we should only exhaust ourselves.' He sat down on the trunk of a fallen tree. The others took up positions, either on the tree or on the ground, to rest. No one spoke. The night was still; the only sound was the distant crackling of the fire.

194

'We'd better get back a bit—I can hear a car coming,' murmured Algy presently.

Biggles sprang to his feet. 'A car!' he echoed. 'At this hour of the morning! I believe you're right, all the same. If you are, that's the answer to our problem. Quick, you fellows, give me a hand with this tree.'

'Losh, what are ye goin' to do wi' it?' demanded Jock in a voice of amazement.

'Throw it across the road,' snapped Biggles. 'That'll stop the car. If it's a private car, it's ours. Give me that pistol Ginger.' Biggles thrust the weapon into his pocket and then helped the others to drag the fallen tree across the road. It was slender, so it entailed no great effort. 'Back under cover, every one, till we see what we've caught,' he ordered.

There was a general rush for the trees as the wavering beams of the car's headlights came over the brow of a rise and probed the darkness ahead, making the pines on either side stand out flat, like stage scenery.

'It's a private car,' whispered Biggles. 'Don't move till I say the word.'

The car began to slow down when the headlights picked out the obstruction on the road, and came to a quiet standstill, with the engine just purring, a few yards short of it. The door was flung open and a man in a smart uniform stepped out. The lights of the car glinted on a row of medals. He looked at the tree, kicked it, and tried to move it, but it was too much for him. He called out something in an angry voice, whereupon a second officer got out of the car and came to his assistance.

'Now,' hissed Biggles, and darted forward. 'Hands up!' he snapped, not caring whether the words were

195

understood or not. The pointed muzzle of a pistol is an argument understood anywhere, by any one.

The two motorists sprang round in affright, as they had good reason to, and then slowly raised their hands. Taken completely by surprise, there was nothing else they could do. They stared wonderingly at the five wild figures confronting them. Jock alone—unshaven, hair tousled, a club-like length of pinewood in his hand—was enough to frighten any one.

'Do you speak English?' asked Biggles curtly.

'*Si*—yes. Who are you? What is zis?' was the equally curt response.

'I'm sorry, gentlemen, but I need your car,' said Biggles, his eyes noting the wings on the officer's breast, and drawing swift conclusions from them. 'I shall also need your tunics, and your caps,' he added.

One of the officers snorted a protest, but Biggles silenced him. 'I have already apologized, gentlemen, but circumstances permit no other course. As an officer myself—flying officer—I feel for you, but—it is war. We are prisoners. We are escaping—and, I may say, we are desperate. Whether you agree or not, we shall have what we need. Will you give them to us, or must we employ methods that are—undignified?'

One of the officers shrugged his shoulders in a manner which conveyed as much as he could have said, and slowly took off his tunic. The other, muttering under his breath, did the same.

Biggles took off their straight-peaked caps, bowed, and stepped back a pace. 'It is with real regret that I must leave you to walk,' he said, and moved towards the car.

Ginger hurried to his side. 'What about the telegraph wires?' he whispered. 'Wouldn't it be safer to cut them?

There are houses lower down the road. They may have a telephone.'

'Yes, cut them,' agreed Biggles shortly.

Ginger ran to the nearest telegraph pole, but Summers ran after him. He had guessed Ginger's intention.

'Gimme them pliers; I'll soon 'ave 'em down,' he declared. He took the pliers from Ginger's hand and went up the pole like a monkey. Four sharp twangs and as many wires fell to the ground. He came down—looking more than ever like a monkey—and they rejoined Biggles at the car. Jock and Algy had dragged the tree aside.

'*Buenos noches, señores; gracias*!*' Biggles bowed and got into the driving-seat of the car. Algy got in beside him; the others piled in behind. The car moved forward smoothly, leaving the two coatless officers in the road.

'Blimey! This way for Marble Arch,' chuckled Summers. 'A bit o' luck, eh?'

'It's time we had a bit,' Ginger told him. 'It wasn't all luck, anyway. If Biggles hadn't—'

'Don't talk so much,' broke in Biggles. 'Keep your eyes open and be ready to move smartly. We've some way to go, and anything can happen before we get to the aerodrome. We've got to find it, anyway. Are we going right, Jock?'

'Ah think so. Speakin' fra' memory, there's only one road in these parts, and the aerodrome's beside it. What d'ye reckon to do wi' yon pretty jackets?'

'Put 'em on in a minute,' returned Biggles. 'We shall at least look like officers, and not like a gang of toughs—at least, two of us will. For once, things are fitting in nicely, I believe. This car coming down the road wasn't

* Good night, gentlemen, thank you

197

an accident. It was going to the aerodrome. I've travelled down a road in a car at this hour of the morning many a time; and when I have, it has always been with the same object.'

'Ye mean—?'

'What time do bombers usually bomb your back areas?'

'Aboot dawn.'

'That's what I thought. That's the usual time. Afterwards they can rumble home and land in daylight. We ought to arrive at the aerodrome in nice time to find a formation of bombers getting ready to take off. That suits us very well. The chances are that the two fellows we stopped sleep out, and come to the aerodrome regularly in this car; which means that the arrival of this car won't cause any surprise. If Algy and I wear the borrowed tunics it should help the deception. If we are going to be hanged—and we shall be if they catch us— it may as well be for a sheep as a lamb. That is always one advantage of being absolutely desperate: you take chances which otherwise would sound awful. When nothing you can do can make things worse, it really saves you a lot of worry.'

For twenty minutes the car raced on. There were no side turnings, so there was no risk of losing the way. They passed an occasional farm-house, and the head-quarters at which Biggles and Algy had been interrogated the previous afternoon, but at that hour in the morning they were silent. There was a sentry on duty at the entrance to the head-quarters, but he barely glanced up as the car raced by.

The hills on either side had now given way to open, treeless country, and the reason for the location of the aerodrome became apparent.

'How much farther, Jock?' asked Biggles.

'I'm not sure, but it canna be far,' was the reply.

A minute or two later the roar of an aero engine being run up confirmed his belief. As Biggles slowed down, the car breasted a slight fold in the ground and the black bulk of the hangars came into view. Lights were everywhere. They reflected on quickly moving figures, and on a line of six Caproni bombers that stood out in front of the hangars.

Biggles switched off his headlights. 'We've two methods open to us,' he said. 'We can either get out here and try to approach unseen, and so make a rush for a machine, or we can drive straight in and play a big bluff. These people are, I fancy, Italians—or most of them. They've Italian machines, and these uniforms we have are Italian. I expect the mechanics, having been here some time, can speak Spanish as well as Italian, but I can't speak either to any amount, so there will be no question of talking. Algy, you and I will wear the borrowed plumes; the others get on the floor where they can't be seen.'

Biggles stopped the car long enough for this operation to be performed. 'Now,' he said quietly, 'we'll make for the end machine on the right. I believe the props are already ticking over—I think they all are, if it comes to that, but there will probably be fewer people at the end of the line. We shall drive right up. These are the orders for the instant I stop. Algy, you'll take the left-hand chock, yank it away, and then get aboard. Ginger, you'll do the same with the right-hand chock. Jock and Summers and I will have to clear the machine, both inside and out, wherever the mechanics happen to be. There may be none, but as the engines are running it's pretty certain that there will be at least

199

one fellow there—probably in the cockpit. It's neck or nothing, so if anybody tries to stop us, let 'em have it. Is that clear?'

There was a low chorus of assent.

Biggles, transformed in his borrowed uniform, slipped the car into gear. 'Here we go,' he said. 'England, home and beauty.'

'Scotland for ever!' growled Jock from the floor.

A gateway through a barbed-wire fence, with a sentry-box beside it, gave access to the aerodrome. A sentry was on duty. He brought his rifle to the slope as the car went through. Biggles took it straight on down the road, which ran along the rear of the hangars. Reaching the end one, he turned sharp left, which took him to the tarmac. A number of mechanics were hurrying about on various duties. They took no notice of the car. Out of the corner of his eye Biggles saw a group of leather-clad pilots smoking a last cigarette before the flight. He took no more notice of them. His eyes were riveted on the selected machine, for the ease or difficulty of the rest of their project rested on the number of mechanics with whom they would have to deal.

He had not expected to be stopped, but he experienced a slight thrill of surprise, almost unreality, as he brought the car to a stop as close to the Caproni as he dared go. This, necessarily, was behind the wing, so that the car would not be in the way of the machine taking off. The unfortunate part of this position was, however, he could not see into the control cabin. To get into such a position he would have to go forward of the wing, but as this would involve loss of time he did not do it.

A sleepy-eyed mechanic in dirty overalls was leaning

against the trailing edge of the wing near the cabin door. He straightened himself slowly as Biggles jumped out of the car and went towards him. He looked mildly puzzled at seeing a strange officer, but nothing more. Biggles' fist flew out with all the weight he could put behind it. It caught the man fairly under the jaw, and he went down like an empty sack falling off a shelf.

Without another glance at him, Biggles sprang into the cabin and went forward to the cockpit.

A single mechanic was sitting in the pilot's seat, gazing with languid eyes at the dials on the instrument board, clearly unaware that anything unusual was happening. His first intimation of this was when Biggles' hand closed over his throat from behind and jerked him from the seat.

Biggles flung him into the arms of McLannoch, who was just behind. 'Take care of him,' he shouted, and then got into the seat; his hand closed over the throttle. Looking down through the side window, he was in time to see Algy and Ginger running back, dragging the chocks. Twisting round in his seat, he saw McLannoch and Summers sitting on the Italian mechanic. Algy, panting, pushed past them, and sank into the seat beside him. 'All clear,' he gasped.

'Ginger in?'

'Yes.'

Biggles pushed the throttle slowly forward. The engines roared. The big machine moved slowly forward. There was no wind, so the direction of the take-off did not matter. Swiftly gathering speed, the heavy bomber roared on across the darkened aerodrome. The tail lifted. The joystick in Biggles' right hand became rigid. He eased it back, gently. The vibration of the wheels ceased as the Caproni nosed its way up into the star-spangled sky. Slowly its nose swung round to the north, and remained there.

Biggles found the watch on the instrument board, and his eyes flickered slightly with surprise. It was later than he thought—twenty minutes to four. He glanced at Algy, and saw that he was watching him.

Algy leaned over. 'How far are we from France?' he yelled.

Biggles thought for a moment, trying to visualize the map. 'Between seventy and a hundred miles to the Pyrenees,' he answered.

Algy pointed towards the right-hand side window of the cabin. It was grey with the first pallid flush of dawn. He knew what Algy meant to convey. It would take them half an hour to reach the frontier, and they would have to cross it in daylight. He said nothing, but flew on, still climbing in order to clear the peaks that lay ahead.

Slowly the grey turned to pink, and then to egg-shell blue. Ahead, seemingly close, but still many miles away, the jagged outline of the Pyrenees cut into the blue like a row of broken teeth.

Biggles tapped Algy on the arm. 'Tell Ginger to get into the gunner's place and keep watch behind,' he said. He knew that it was unlikely that there would be a Franco aerodrome in front of them, for they were getting a long way from the theatre of war, so any danger would come from the rear, from the fast inter-ceptor Fiats that might be sent after them.

Algy went aft. He was away for some minutes. 'There are five machines behind us,' he announced calmly. 'They look like Fiats.'

Biggles nodded. 'How far away?'

'Two to three miles.'

202

Biggles' eyes rested thoughtfully on the mountains ahead. Beyond them they would be safe. They were, he judged, twenty miles away. He made no comment, but moved the control column forward a little for maximum speed, turning his nose slightly towards what appeared to be one of the several passes through the mountains.

Five minutes later rolling foothills lay below; the mountains themselves, gaunt and stark, raised an impressive line of peaks just ahead.

Algy, who had again gone aft, returned. 'They're closing up,' he said.

'Has Ginger got a machine-gun?'

'No. I suppose the gunner brought his own gun with him.'

Biggles nodded, and opening the side window, craned his neck in an attempt to see the pursuing machines, but could not, from which he knew that they must be directly behind. He could now see clearly the pass which he had chosen. The opening was not more than a mile away, although how far it extended he had no means of knowing. Another five minutes would see them comparatively safe. Seeing that he still had a few hundred feet of height to spare, he thrust the joystick forward for a final dash. Simultaneously, faintly above the roar of the engines came the crisp chatter of a machine-gun.

Biggles pressed his right foot on the rudder bar; then the left. The machine swayed drunkenly. Again came the *taca-taca-taca* of a machine-gun, and an instant later a Fiat zoomed ahead, having overshot its dive.

Biggles swerved away, but did not take his eyes off it. He saw its nose swing round; saw the bright orange flecks of flame dancing from the muzzle of its guns.

There was nothing he could do, for the mouth of the pass yawned in front of him. A burst of bullets rained on the Caproni as it plunged into the chasm that split the range. One of the engines coughed, coughed again, and went dead, smoking. The bomber roared on, Biggles pressing on the joystick to overcome the torque of the single engine.

A short distance ahead the floor of the pass rose abruptly, forming a ridge. It seemed that the Caproni would not be able to clear it. Biggles eased the stick back, but with a shake of his head allowed it to go forward again as the controls went slack with the threat of an impending stall.

The Caproni rushed towards the rocks. Biggles could see every detail clearly. He could see a double gateway, with the little square huts of the customs people, and knew that it was the frontier. They appeared to swoop towards him. What had happened to the Fiats he neither knew nor cared. They no longer mattered.

With every nerve taut, he steading the stick—eased it back ever so slightly. The machine responded, but its wheels were less than fifty feet from the rising ground, and the frontier a hundred yards ahead. Guards were rushing out of their huts, some to throw themselves flat, others to rush for the shelter of the rocks.

The machine could not do it—Biggles knew that—at least, not in flight. There was one last chance that it might get across, however, and he took it.

With his wheels ten feet from the ground, he jerked the stick back suddenly; then he thrust it forward.

The Caproni reared like a wounded horse. Slowly, with a sickening roll, it wallowed towards the ground in an uncontrolled stall. The instant before its wheels struck, Biggles, with a swift movement of his left hand, flicked off the ignition. The wheels struck. The machine bounded. There was a splintering crash as it came down again on the brightly painted gates of the frontier, scattering them in a cloud of matchwood.

Then came the long grinding crash of the machine itself. It tore through the second gates, smashed a wing-tip against a white pole carrying the red, white, and blue tricolour of France, and cartwheeled over and over down a steep slope on the other side. The wings collapsed in a tangle of wood, wire, and fabric. The fuselage rolled over three times, and then, sticking its nose into a huge boulder beside the track, came to a stop. All noise ceased. Utter silence reigned.

Biggles, half-dazed, kicked out the remains of the side window, and having thus made an exit, turned to see what had happened to the others.

Algy, white-faced, a trickle of blood on his lips, was groping about him wildly. Biggles pushed him through the exit, and then fought his way through splinters of debris to the cabin. Ginger was already half-way out through the gunner's cockpit, which the iron gun-ring had prevented from being crushed. McLannoch, Summers, and the Italian mechanic, all looking not a little scared, were trying to get to their feet. 'Get out,' yelled Biggles. 'She may go on fire yet.' There was nothing he could do inside, so he scrambled back to the control cabin, and so through the window to the ground outside. Fiats were still circling high overhead. They could not get lower on account of the towering rocks on either side of the pass. From the splintered gates of the French frontier post men in French uniform were running towards the crash. Biggles helped the others out of the wreck, and then sat down on a burst tyre to wait for them.

Summers joined him, feeling himself tenderly. 'I knew I shouldn't like this flying game,' he announced ruefully. 'It's worse than the roundabouts on 'Ampstead 'Eath on a bank holiday.'

Biggles smiled, and then stood up to meet the gesticulating frontier guards and customs officers. It took him some minutes to calm them. The discovery that they were British did more in this direction than anything Biggles could say.

He took off his tunic and handed it to the N.C.O. in charge of the post with a little bow. 'A souvenir, monsieur,' he said smiling. Algy did the same.

'I must take you to the officer in charge of my section for examination,' announced the N.C.O. apologetically.

'That will suit me very well,' Biggles told him, in his own language.

The little party set off down the hill.

Chapter 20
Adios—and Au Revoir

There is little more to tell. Once in France, although there were formalities to be complied with involving a little delay, there was no further danger to be feared. By the courtesy of the officials, Biggles was permitted to put through a telephone call to the British Embassy in Paris, as a result of which railway tickets were provided to enable them to reach the French capital, where they were met by a member of the staff to whom Biggles imparted the information that he had a document of the greatest importance to deliver to the Foreign Office in London. Communication between the Embassy in Paris and London expedited their departure, so that on the third day after their crash they were provided with identity cards. Biggles had been in touch with his bank, so, once more properly dressed, they took their places in the midday 'plane for Croydon.

There a car awaited them, and they were taken direct to Whitehall. The others sat in a waiting-room while Biggles, as spokesman of the party, was conducted elsewhere. It was an hour before he rejoined them.

'Well, that's that—thank goodness,' he announced. 'And now, what about a bite of real food somewhere?'

'Here! Just a minute,' broke in Ginger. 'What did they say?'

'Who?'

'The fellow—or people—you just saw.'

'Oh, nothing.'

'*Nothing?*'

'Well, I told them just what happened—and one or two other things which I thought would interest them.'

'And they said *nothing?*'

'Well, they said, "Thanks very much." What else did you expect them to say?'

'After all the messes we got in over their perishing letter—by the way, what was in it?'

Biggles shook his head. 'I haven't the remotest idea,' he answered lightly.

'Do you mean to say they didn't tell you?'

'You bet your life they didn't. But they've agreed to pay our out-of-pocket expenses—and when the British government does that you can reckon that they are very much obliged to you. That's right, Jock, isn't it?'

'Ye're dead richt—but they did once gi' me a tin medal.'

'They once gave me a week in jug for loiterin' wivout invisible means of substance,' growled Summers.

Biggles laughed. Then he became serious. 'No, chaps,' he said, as they walked slowly towards the exit, 'it's just because any Britisher would do what we've done that the old Empire goes on. I've done what I set out to do, so what have I got to grumble about, anyway?'

'What was that?' asked Algy. 'It's so long ago that I've forgotten.'

'I've got rid of my fever,' murmured Biggles, and then whistled a passing taxi. 'Café Royal,' he told the driver, and crowding in with the others, slammed the door.